In Wild Lemon Groves

BY

SELINA KRAY

This is a work of fiction. Names, characters, places, and incidents are either the product of the author's imagination or used fictitiously. Any resemblance to actual persons living or dead, business establishments, events, or locales is entirely coincidental.

In Wild Lemon Groves
Copyright © 2017 by Selina Kray
Cover Art: Tiferet Design (www.TiferetDesign.com)
Editor: Nancy-Anne Davies
ISBN: 978-09959925-3-5
eBook ISBN: 978-09959925-2-8

All rights reserved. No part of this book may be reproduced or transmitted in any form or by any means, electronic or mechanical, including photocopying, recording, or by any information storage and retrieval system without the written permission of the author, and where permitted by law. Reviewers may quote brief passages in a review. To request permission, and for all other inquiries, contact the author at selinakray@hotmail.ca.

First Edition
February 2018

Dedication

*To Susie, Sally, and Maribeth,
for the magnificent dinners, the starlight debates,
holding my hand through the brush fires,
and sharing your Amalfi with me*

Chapter One

SCENT OF SEA AND PALM,
CRAGGY AND ANCIENT, A WORLD
BATHED IN SAFFRON
- #17, *IN BLUE SOLITUDES*, S. WILSON-OSAKI

"*A*. S'okay." Bleary eyed and bone weary, Sébastien stared at the sign for two minutes before it registered. He kept his distance, glanced around the bushel of sun-ripened cab drivers and chauffeurs waiting to squeeze every last euro out of their charges, but no.

This was him. Smile so bright it blinded, like glare off a windshield. Footballer's frame decked in team colors and too-tight shorts. Face Bernini could have sculpted. Hair black as an oil slick, greased into a neat, perfect slope. His tortoiseshell eyes twinkled in Seb's direction when he took a cautious step forward.

"*Signor* S'okay?"

"Osaki. Yes."

"Ah, Osokay."

"Osaki. O-sak-i. Japanese."

"You fly from Japan?"

"No. Canada. Montreal."

"*Si, si, Signor* Osaki. Sebastiano."

Seb opened his mouth to correct him but nodded instead. "That's me."

"Andrea Sorrentino." He thumped a hand on his chest. "You want I take your bag?"

"Uh…"

Before he could decide, the driver clacked down the handle on his extra-fee-heavy suitcase and hefted it under his arm like an unruly toddler. "*Vieni, vieni.*" He dove into the crowd before Seb could get his bearings.

Spotting the clean line to the exit, Seb set his own pace, his tipsy head still mired in a post-flight fugue. Thirty-two sleepless hours, plus a morning spent tracing and retracing his path through the labyrinthine halls of the Rome airport to make his connection, left him listless. With exhaustion but also nerves. What had he been thinking, shipping off to a country he'd never been to and where he didn't speak the language?

The answer, of course, was Henry. Who should have been there, propping him up with his rock climber's arms, but also with his wonderment, the kid-in-a-candy store way he'd seen the world. Henry had puffed all his energy and excitement and fire into Seb's lead balloon and—in his latest impossible feat—made him fly.

Clutching his backpack like a life preserver, Seb practiced his deep breathing as he waded through the stream of travellers. More of a trickle, really, now that he was in the flow. One foot in front of the other, he reminded himself, looking for a focal point. A taut jean-clad ass, with a carefree swagger all its own, lured him the rest of the way. Seb staggered out of the airport terminal...

... into a whole new world. The hazy afternoon sun swaddled him like a warm blanket. Ripe with the scent of palm trees and petrol, the parking lot was more social gathering than frantic hub, with drivers chatting, smoking, and laughing as they waited for clueless travellers to wander by. Stoic mountains—silent sentries at the gate to paradise—shadowed the horizon, rings of mist crowning their crater heads.

Woozy with relief, Seb lowered his lids to half-mast and basked in the moment. This was Henry's world. He was safe.

A hulking black SUV screeched to a halt in front of him, blocking the view. Before Seb could decide whether to be terrified or outraged, his driver slid open the side door, beckoning him into his luxury air-conditioned chariot. Too polite to give in to the urge to collapse across the seats and zonk out, Seb stumbled into the nearest chair. His hands shook as he fought with the seat belt. Something about that fateful click brought the reality back home—he was trapped in a jet-fuelled coffin with a man who could barely pronounce his name, soon to be zipping down a highway where speed limits weren't even guidelines, thousands of miles from home, by a world-famous volcano that once scorched everything for miles—

Hand on his knee. There was a hand on his knee.

"*Signor* Osakay? You want I get you espresso? Water? Food? Is no trouble."

"No." Seb shut his eyes, sucked in all the air he could. "I... I'm just tired. Didn't sleep on the plane." When he opened them again, he met soft eyes shimmering with kindness. His exhalation came easy. So did his smile. What was his name again? Andrea Sorrentino. A gentle name, full of music.

"Granita al limone. Un momento." A squeeze to Seb's knee, and he hopped out the door.

Andrea returned a few minutes later with a small plastic cup half-filled with yellow slush. A DayGlo-green straw canted archly over the rim, the non-business end cut at an angle like stems at the bottom of a vase. At his expectant look, Seb took a quick sip… and jolted back in his seat as tart, tasty goodness ripped across his tongue. He went in for a second, longer draught of the cool lemonade-on-steroids slush, unable to stop from moaning in approval. "On steroids" didn't really do the flavor justice—sweeter and tangier than normal lemonade, the drink was more like gourmet sorbet, though no grain of sugar had ever polluted this nectar. Seb wasn't even a quarter of the way done, and already he wanted another.

"Yes?" Andrea had the look of a puppy begging for its master's approval. Something in his expression silenced the last of Seb's worries.

"Perfect. Thank you."

"Now… to Amalfi?"

"Please."

Seb downed the last of his *granita*—instantly regretting drinking it so fast—as they zoomed onto the highway. Traffic and Andrea's smooth driving helped regulate their speed. Seb soon found his eyes drooping, not helped by the sparse, industrial scenery, the sea and the mountains too far away to impress. Even the ruins of Pompeii, which Andrea excitedly pointed out, looked like a shantytown in any poor country from this distance. But then the Villa of the Mysteries probably wasn't all that mysterious after thousands of years trapped in rubble.

The click-clack of the turn signal ticked down like a timer in his head. Seb swallowed hard, straightened in his seat. A swerve, and the side of one of the not-so-distant mountains blacked out the windshield, its slope soaring up into the clouds. A sharp right turn led to another, the bulky SUV scraping around hairpin corners and playing chicken with the motorbikes that chased it up the narrow roads. Heavy on the horn and light on patience, Andrea barrelled along the dusty paths as if pitchfork-wielding villagers raced him to the summit. Seb bit the side of his tongue to keep from crying out and dropped his gaze into his lap, but that was somehow worse than watching the near misses and almost collisions in action.

"You fly solo, *Signor* Osakay?"

"Uh… yes."

"Long way?"

"Ten hours. Fifteen if you count the layover and getting to the airport."

"Is cold in Montreal?"

Seb would have rolled his eyes if they weren't so busy trying to make sure they hadn't hit anything. Every non-Canadian thought they lived in 24/7, 365-day arctic conditions. "Not in September."

"Is warm?"

"Not like here."

"Ah, here is *bellissimo*." Andrea took his hand off the

steering wheel to gesture at the sun; Seb counted the seconds, fighting to control his heaving breaths. "First time you come to Amalfi?"

"Yes."

"You will like. You have friend?"

"No. Just me." Seb hugged his arms around his backpack, wondering how much he should say. To his driver. A person he had met a half hour before. But then Henry's number-one piece of advice had always been to get to know the locals.

"Just you? I give you cards." To Seb's horror, Andrea wrenched his hips around to dig into his pocket with only his elbow on the wheel. He pulled out a stack of business cards that would not have been out of place at a convention. With maybe half an eye on the road, he flicked through them. Too choked with fear to reprimand him, Seb almost resorted to prayer. "Villa Napolitana... Ah! Very close, Taverna del Duca. You tell them Andrea send you, they give you good meal. Pasta, pizza, fish, all good. Very close to villa." He passed the Taverna's business card back without looking at Seb or the path but somehow managed a 180 turn up at steep hill.

"That's very kind of—"

"In Piazza del Dogi, Ristorante L'Abside. Best pizza in Amalfi. You tell them. Andrea. Also Da Gemma. Same menu from 1872. You know what is Genovese?"

"From Genoa, you mean?"

"*Si*, pasta Genovese. Onions, meat, wine, cooked long time. Don't miss."

"Any seafood? Fish?"

"Everywhere. Everywhere in Amalfi. So fresh, still move, eh?" Andrea's smile was just distracting enough to make Seb forget they played bumper cars on a road used to ferrying horse-drawn carts. One way. "For special night, Marina Grande." Andrea plucked two more cards out of his pack. "What you like? Prawns? *Polpo*? Lobster?"

"All of it." Seb would have murdered a huge bowl of seafood pasta if his stomach weren't currently lodged in his throat.

"*Bene.* Where else you go?"

By the time the SUV hit a flat stretch near the summit, Seb had a full deck of recommendations, each suit capped with the Italian version of "you'll get a discount if you tell them I sent you." Seb doubted the sincerity of this but not of the man himself. With his easy smile and eagerness to help, he would remember the warmth of Andrea's welcome long after memories of minor inconveniences had faded. With the windows down and the wind ruffling his slick locks back into curls, Seb thought he caught a glimpse of the man beneath the manscaping. He soon realized it was the same guy he'd been seeing all along. Andrea's enthusiasm for people was as genuine as his love for his little Campania town, and Seb happily lost himself in their conversation.

Until the view caught him up short. They circled around a dead-drop valley, stunning if Seb dared to look down. A chandelier of mist hovered in midair, dripping its crystalline wisps down the mountains' décolletage. He gaped until they rounded the far side of the second mountain, and then… the sea. An indescribable ribbon of blue stretching out to the gauzy horizon. The color of the serenity he searched for.

The color of Henry's eyes. All at once Seb understood why his husband insisted he see this place, stand on a beach where every pebble was kissed by history and stare out into the Tyrrhenian blue.

Henry blue.

"*Magnifico*, no?"

A bobsled run down the latest slope shot Seb back to the present. And his terror of not making it to his villa alive.

"There are no words." Or none he'd care to share. He scoured his mind for another of Henry's tips. Ah, yes. Get people talking. "How long have you lived here?"

"Always. My father, he drive since I was little…" He patted an invisible child's head. "Then we do together. Now is me."

"He's retired?"

A few heartbeats of silence, and Seb cursed his stupidity.

"No. Cancer. Too much smoking."

Swallowing back a surge of emotion, Seb rasped out, "I'm so sorry. I shouldn't have asked…"

Andrea's shrug caught him by surprise. "Is life. I drive for him, sister take care of Mamma. Italian way."

But Seb couldn't leave it, couldn't escape the words that burned on his tongue every minute of every day for the past three years. Their fumes wet his eyes and choked off his breath, same as the moment the police knocked on his door. Maybe if he confessed them to this gentle, happy man, his jollity would finally douse their fire.

"I lost my husband." The words were out before he knew what to do with them, hanging in the air like the mist between the mountains. "That's why I'm here alone. It's… It would have been our tenth anniversary."

Gray-green eyes met his in the rear-view mirror, and the world stilled. The jostle of the SUV as it screeched around another corner, the suffocating humidity that poured in through the windows, the epic view and the weight of Andrea's admission all fell away as their gazes met. Seb saw nothing but the deepest compassion in Andrea's glinting eyes.

"He is here with you. His *spirito*."

Seb filled his lungs with sea air, nodded. "More than you know." He dug into his backpack, pulled out Henry's book. A few pictures threatened to spill out, but Seb tucked them back in. "He was a travel writer. Guidebooks. For Lonely Planet. This was one of his favorite places. I have all his notes. All the stuff he couldn't fit in the book."

"Ah, then you tell me a little lie, *Signor* Osakay. This trip you are not alone."

For the first time in a long, long time, Seb found his smile.

"No. I guess not."

The SUV screeched to a halt in front of a pair of towering iron doors better suited to a bank vault than vacation apartments. The dregs of Seb's *granita* buzz wouldn't have fuelled a fly. He tumbled out onto the stone sidewalk, stared up at the fortress-like walls that protected the Villa

Napolitana from the ravening hordes of tourists. Granted, the cardigan-clad seniors and hand-holding newlyweds that clogged the main street hadn't looked all that mercenary except when clamoring for a good deal, but Seb appreciated the extra layer of privacy all the same.

Until Andrea swung open one of the doors, revealing a staircase that put the 491 steps to the top of St. Peter's Basilica to shame. Or so it seemed to Seb, who seriously considered asking Andrea to throw him over his shoulder—as he now did with Seb's suitcase—and gallop up the steps with the ease of an Italian greyhound. Not even Andrea's succulent ass could tempt him into action. He heaved his backpack onto his shoulders, not quite Atlas bearing the weight of the world, but close. Seb crawled up the first few steps to the small landing behind the doors and considered curling up in a shadowy corner with the slinky little tabby hiding there.

"*Vattene*, Andrea!" With a hiss and a clap in the cat's direction, Andrea came bounding down again. "*Fila!*"

Seb's exhausted mind processed this as slowly as the cat uncoiled itself, stretched, and ambled away. "He's an Andrea too?"

"*Sì.*" The full force of his thousand-ampere smile bedazzled Seb anew. "Sant' Andrea sleep in the Duomo. You know, we pass. He is *santo patrono* of Amalfi. Many, many people have this name."

"And animals, I guess."

His musical laugh almost lulled Seb into a trance. "Yes, many. *Piccolo* Andrea live in the *supermercato*. He catch the mice. But here there are birds, people…"

"Treats and cuddles."

"He stay too long, not do his job. His mamma no like."

Seb poorly stifled a yawn. "But I think he had the right idea." He slumped down onto one of the steps, a wind-up toy that needed a good crank. And wasn't that the truth?

"Ah, *signore!* You want I help?" Andrea swallowed a laugh, proffered an arm.

As inviting as that tan, toned support looked, Seb clung white-knuckled to his dignity.

"Call me Seb."

"Eh?"

"Sébastien. Seb. No one who's put up with me like this should call me 'sir.'"

"Sebastiano, *si.*" The brightness of Andrea's grin could have powered a small village. Seb wondered if everyone in this country was so high voltage. "Lucia, she wait with your key. You want I take your bag?"

Seb gripped the straps of his backpack, glanced up the endless staircase. Even in the shade, his skin slurped up the day's humidity like a sponge, leaving him clammy and bloated. His breaths heaved with moisture like a trout slow drowning on dry land. A dull percussion beat on the backs of his eyes, war drums signalling an incoming migraine. And here before him, his own personal Mercury, ready to wing his belongings up to Olympus.

"Please." He slipped off his backpack, which made standing much easier. Once shed, its weight somehow tripled—he barely managed to keep it a foot off the ground as he handed it off to Andrea. To his surprise, his godly companion didn't wing off into the clouds, but matched his pace as Seb tackled the steps.

Too winded for polite conversation, he was relieved when Andrea launched into a narration of the property's virtues. The website photos hadn't deceived: the sun-swept three-story building with wrought-iron terraces and a red slat roof slotted into a succession of fieldstone-speckled ledges that had been carved out of the mountainside. Green with dense shrubbery and gray with old igneous rock, the mountain loomed over the Villa Napolitana like a sleeping giant.

At a peak-a-boo archway in the garden wall, Seb stopped cold—not to wheeze, but to gasp. A teardrop-shaped pool nestled in a bed of grass. On the far side, a grove of thin-trunked, bushy-leaved trees sheltered two rows of chaise longues. A simple wood gate underscored a breathtaking view of inner Amalfi, the full-bloom sun hanging over their giant peak's twin. Seb estimated he had just enough energy left for a sprint and a cannonball into the beguiling waters.

Instead he turned back toward an equally beguiling sight: Andrea, eyes glinting with knowing and mischief.

"I think I've come to the right place."

With what Seb would come to recognize as a classic Italian shrug, Andrea steered him back toward the stairs. "Your *amante* would not send you wrong."

Seb attempted a laugh; it came out more like a cough. "I chose this place. The company he worked for paid for all his expenses. I had to be more…"

"*Frugale.*"

"Exactly."

As he lumbered up the last flight, Andrea hovering behind as if to break his fall, the heat and humidity and stress and jet lag waged a full-on assault on his senses. Seb swayed, cursed, steadied himself. The final three steps stretched up like hurdles in his mind's eye. He *would not* pass out, he inwardly scolded himself, in front of the first man whose smile he could bear without feeling like an adulterous worm.

A gentle touch—or was it a wisp of breeze—nudged the small of Seb's back. Closing his eyes, he summoned up the strength to climb one, two, three calf-straining steps to… a lovely little terrace with a cozy table for four and a higher angle on the spectacular view. Spellbound, at first he didn't notice the short bottle blonde with the round face and the peppy Jack Russell terrier.

The dog soon made itself known, lunging for Andrea, who dropped to his knees and welcomed him like a long-lost child.

"*Signor* Osakay? I am Lucia Barroso, manager of the Villa Napolitana."

"And this is Matto," Andrea said between furious licks to his face. "He is a bit…" Another shrug. "But very nice."

Seb offered the dog his hand for sniffing, but he was no match for Andrea.

"You are in number three, *signore*." Lucia gestured toward the furthest of three doors at the very end of the terrace. "I'll show you."

Seb nodded but couldn't quite pry away from the sight of Andrea cooing at and caressing Matto, who revved up further with each pet—a miniature rocket ready to launch into the stratosphere. Lucia whistled, and the little dog wriggled out of Andrea's arms and trotted to her side, leaving Seb to stare dumbly at the man who was, after all, only his driver. Not, say, a life preserver he could cling to for the rest of the trip.

"Well..." Seb cleared his throat. "Thank you. For everything."

"I see you in the piazza." He handed over his backpack; Seb didn't think he imagined the lingering brush of his fingers. "Amalfi very small. We say '*buongiorno.*' You tell me what you do. In your book."

"I will."

"You remember. *Granita al limone.*"

Seb found his smile. "How could I forget something so *deliziosa?*"

Andrea's laugh echoed up through the valley and over the mountains.

Chapter Two

Chapel bell tower,
A corona of starlight,
Enchanted evening
-#38, *In Blue Solitudes*, S. Wilson-Osaki

Seb shivered, burrowed deeper under the duvet. An unfamiliar vinegary scent tickled his nose. The pillow under his cheek felt too springy for comfort, the sheets too silky—not his usual flannel. He snaked a hand under the covers, seeking out Henry's solidity and warmth, but his fingers skidded off the edge of the bed. He curled his arm back into his cocoon, remembering.

Not where he was, but who he was. A widower. An astronaut floating through the vacuum of space, untethered to any place or thing. A cowardly lion. He curled his legs into his chest, listened. The breathy hum of an air conditioner explained the glacial temperature. Distant voices cackled over some unknown joke. A flapping noise, the honk of a horn, a motor buzzing, the thwap-thwap of sandals on tile.

Amalfi, waiting for him.

Seb lifted the duvet an inch, peered out. His apartment in the Villa Napolitana was a humble but pristine paradise.

Shades of white with Mediterranean-blue accents. Shuttered windows framed by sunlight raring to burst in. Exposed beams steepled into a vaulted ceiling. Through the rail that lined the loft bedroom, a school of ceramic fish swam across the living room wall.

Everything post-Andrea was a blur. Lucia must have given him the grand tour. He must have climbed up to the loft, unpacked his suitcase, and crawled into bed without passing Go. Seb flipped the top edge of the duvet back, eyeballed his alarm clock: 10:00 a.m. He had slept for twenty hours straight.

Certain neglected bodily functions suddenly made themselves known to him, and he half staggered, half tumbled his way to the bathroom. He stared at the bidet for a full thirty seconds before his bladder gave him no choice in the matter. Once relieved, Seb leered at the shower as if the entire All Blacks rugby team had piled into the glass stall. He stripped. Once scrubbed of airplane germs and shorn of his tumbleweed beard, he felt almost ready to tackle the coffee maker.

Then he remembered he was in Italy, where java flowed thick and hot as Vesuvius's lava, and threw on some clothes.

He stepped out into a world so gilt and ancient it was practically sepia-toned. The sun god had scorched off all the previous day's humidity. The warm air enveloped him but wasn't heavy, fragrant with sea salt and citrus grove. Two storeys below, the lost-earring pool glimmered—so inviting—but for the first time in three years, Seb wanted to explore. Even if it meant tackling those stairs, which hadn't gotten less intimidating from the top down.

A wolf whistle sounded from the far end of the terrace.

Three tanned and freckled middle-aged ladies sat around a table, a game of poker in full swing. A seashell necklace had been sacrificed for chips; three sentry espresso cups guarded their stashes. Though they all wore sunglasses, two of them scoped him out while the third ground her cigarette into an ashtray and quickly lit up another.

"And who might you be, new neighbor?" With her bushel of strawberry hair and beaming smile, she looked about as threatening as Anne of Green Gables.

"Seb. Uh, I mean, Sébastien." He shuffled in their direction but hesitated to commit.

"First day?" This from a bronze-skinned woman with cornrows who wouldn't have looked out of place wielding a spear.

"Second, technically."

"Well, welcome to paradise!" She nudged back the free chair with her knee. "Have a seat. Get your bearings."

"Uh… do you have coffee?"

The redhead sprang to her feet. "Only from the cutest little shop in Positano. And you have to try the *sfogliatella*." She herded Seb into his seat before disappearing into their apartment. "I'm Kath, and that's my sister Ceri." The smoker lifted her sunglasses to wink at him. "And this is my bestie Maya. Whereabouts are you from, Seb?"

"Canada. Montreal."

"Told you," Ceri drawled. Black Irish to her sister's red, she had the hair and the attitude of a Jackie Onassis.

Sliding two of her seashells over, Maya asked, "Is that close to Edmonton? We met a couple from there in Rome."

"Not really, no. Montreal is more like Boston, and Edmonton is more like Albuquerque."

Maya's laughed bubbled up like a fountain. "I see you've guessed we're American."

"Hard not to," Ceri said, emphasizing her Southern accent. Seb guessed Louisiana.

"Not to mention the hospitality." Seb forgot the conversation the instant Kath plunked his espresso under his nose, along with a rippled shell-shaped pastry that wrung an eager gurgle from his long-empty stomach. He accepted a fork to keep from devouring it. "Thank you for this."

"Old habits." Kath chuckled. "Miss my kids. Don't get me wrong, I'm grateful for the me time…"

"… as long as she has someone to feed," Maya finished. "You may live to regret that sfoglia-whatsits."

Seb, whose mouth sung with flakey, creamy, orange zesty perfection, vigorously shook his head. The ladies trilled and cooed as if they'd taken in a lost puppy. Seb had to admit there was some truth to the comparison. Then he sipped his espresso, deciding he needed some alone time with their coffeemaker.

"Is there a Mrs. Seb?" Maya asked, with a sphinxlike smile.

He swallowed hard. He hated this part. Too many land mines, each one waiting to blow up a new friendship before it started.

"No. On my own for this one. Or, well… from now on."

"Oh, honey." Kath was as full-on with her sympathy as her breakfast sharing, taking his free hand and squeezing her support into his palm. "Was it a breakup or the big D?"

Ceri scoffed. "Nosy parker."

"No, no, it's..." Seb eyed the rest of his pastry longingly, wondering if he could scarf it before he had to admit the truth. He was stereotyping, he knew, but it was an election year, and the Southern states did have something of a reputation. "The biggest D of all. The final D, you might say. My husband Henry, a few years ago." A hundred and two million heartbeats, to be exact. Not that Seb was counting.

All three of them stilled, stared at him. Seb braced for rudeness or rejection, already warning himself that he would not let an incident ruin his vacation. Then the ladies shoved out of their seats and encircled him into a group hug so snug he reevaluated his orientation. Seb felt so mothered he was surprised when they let go without pinching his cheeks. But then he suspected they didn't want to grab the ones on his face.

"You're coming to dinner with us," mama bear Kath pronounced with a solemnity that made Seb wonder if he'd be sent to his room if he defied her. Considering that's where he'd planned to spend most evenings, it wouldn't be much of a punishment. "We found the perfect little trattoria."

"Down one of the side alleys," Maya continued. "If you have some extra time, it's worth it to check them out. We found a few hidden gems and, oh, the villas!"

"Maybe he has plans for the day," Ceri interjected. "Like we do."

"I don't want to be any bother—" Seb stammered.

"Don't be silly," Kath reassured him, shooting her sister a look Maya cosigned. "We're just off to Maiori for the afternoon. We'll be back and in the pool by five."

Maya nodded. "And what are your plans for the day, cher?"

"To be honest, I hadn't thought any further than coffee."

Ceri barked out a laugh. "Sounds about right. Should I deal you in, or are you itching to get going?"

"What's your game?"

"Oxford stud."

"Just like my first boyfriend." The ladies cackled as Seb savored the last bite of *sfogliatella*. "I'll play a round."

"Oh, honey," Kath sighed, pink cheeked from laughing. "You're a keeper."

Seb fingered the cottony pages of his new leather-bound journal, traced the initials embossed on the cover: S.W.O. Sébastien Wilson-Osaki. He hadn't planned on marring the pristine pages with his half-formed thoughts. Hadn't planned on splurging on such a fancy journal, but the gift shop of the paper-making museum was packed with so many goodies that Seb couldn't help filling his bag. He'd also bought a photo album decorated with dried wildflowers, another flower-laden strip of handmade paper to be framed, and a personalized stamp.

The words hadn't come until he parked at one of the boardwalk cafés, ostensibly to people watch until his pizza came. The dank smell of the drying pulp still twitched his nose, the churn of the eleventh-century press echoed in his ears, and the view before him… well. It hardly took a poet to find it inspiring.

But a poet Seb was. The bustling marina, the flowerbed beach, the rows upon rows of pastel houses, the sun shimmer off the Tyrrhenian Sea all worked their magic on his writer's imagination, kindling a desire in him only his fountain pen could quench. That and the parched pages of his journal, which drank in every word that poured out of him with bottomless thirst. The block that had stopped him for well over a year popped off as easily as a champagne cork. He'd started in the middle to keep the first pages clean, to hide his first overeager spurts, no better than his teenage scribblings. But finally something began to take form, to solidify into structure and meaning.

At long last, he had something to say.

In the throes of grief, Seb wrote to stay afloat, to keep from slitting his wrists or sailing off the nearest cliff. An entire library's worth of sentimental drivel that first year. But if he kept forming letters into words into sentences, if he bled across pages instead of his bedsheets, he could ignore the emptiness of his house. Of his life. He would fill the Henry-shaped hole with verse after verse, a patchwork of loss that, if he was lucky, might one day become a quilt. Which it had. Seb had wrapped in it so tightly that he'd been trapped in this false comfort. By the first anniversary of Henry's death, he couldn't write. He didn't want to leave the house. He insulated against the judgments and the sympathies of his family and friends. And all those words, all that ink, his grief's masterwork, amounted to nothing more than a pile of rubbish.

He burnt every last page the day he booked his ticket to Amalfi. Dug Henry's notes out of storage and followed his instructions to the letter. Every step he took in this golden place resounded with Henry's approval. But Seb was here to find himself again, to cast a light on the shadow of his husband's death. He scanned over the few pages he'd managed and smiled.

Then his pizza arrived, and his stomach wrenched back the controls.

Once refueled, he set off down the other side of the boardwalk, which extended the length of the docks between three long piers. As mesmerizing as the slow progress of distant cruise liners could be, Seb spent more time gawking at the hillside villas. Rising up in tiers of white and yellow wedding cake shades, with terracotta roofs and vaulted windows, they resembled the storybook houses he'd imagined as a child. Seb wouldn't have been surprised if the population of Amalfi were secretly gnomes or imps impersonating people to trade tourist dollars for fairy dust. The fact that the stone arches that supported the coastal road looked like battlements, complete with castle-like watchtowers at every outward curve, only made the place seem more enchanted.

Only when he returned to the Villa Napolitana did he realize staying at the top of a hill—no matter how slowly he window-shopped up the main street—was a bad move after a day of walking. By the time he crawled up the five thousand steps to his front door, his small shopping bags of supplies sagging as if he carried bowling balls, Seb was ready to spend the rest of his vacation in a zero-gravity chair.

An artfully arranged man-bun and a thin coating of sunscreen later, he clopped back down a few circles of hell to the jewel in the Villa Napolitana's crown: the pool. He creaked through the gate to discover Kath, Ceri, and Maya already lounging on the shallow end steps, a floating bar tray bobbing between them. Seb dropped his towel on one of the aforementioned chairs, abandoning his journal and flip-flops for the glinting waters.

A chorus of "Seb!" had him feeling self-conscious until he waded into the blue. The water, sun, and soaring peaks inspired the kind of serenity he'd only found twice before: on the shore of Lake Kawaguchi, with a postcard view of Mount Fuji in the distance, and lying in a hammock with Henry on their Hawaiian honeymoon. Henry had written *Make new memories every day* in block letters at the start of his notes, and it pleased Seb to realize he was living this mantra. After a few laps, he swam back to the shallow end underwater, popping up unexpectedly to spook the ladies.

Who chuckled indulgently but didn't stir.

"G&T?" Bartender Ceri asked.

Seb laughed. "Do I have a choice?"

"I can give it to you straight."

"Not my style."

"That makes two of us, cher."

Seb tittered along with them as he parked in a free space on one of the lower steps. Accepting his drink, he turned, as they were, toward the sun. He took a sip and nodded his approval. "Perfection."

"I'll say." Maya lowered her sunglasses to scope someone out. Seb followed her eyeline to a balcony across the street, where an Italian gym bunny was getting frisky with his barbells.

"Is that Gerardo?" Kath purred her Rs. "He's late."

"Must have run out of oil," Seb quipped. "Do you think he bastes, or does it just seep out of his pores?"

"Meow!" Maya exclaimed. "Not your type?"

"He's strokeworthy, but I wouldn't put a ring on it."

"I was thinking more Stella in a *How She Got Her Groove Back* revival."

"Italian edition? I could see it." They clinked glasses. "Your man done you wrong?"

"Every single one of them."

"When they found out about each other," Ceri interjected.

"I try to tell them commitment's not for me. They never listen."

Seb nodded. "Comes with having a dick. Men experience a fifty to seventy percent attention-span reduction when they hit puberty."

"Or, you know, when they're born." Kath snickered. "I have three sons."

"My condolences."

"Thank you. But they are five thousand miles away, and that bottle of good-time juice is still half-full." She shook her glass, then downed the lot. "How about you, handsome? Are you feeling more Angela Bassett or Julia Roberts?"

"Kathleen Gleeson!" Ceri smacked her arm. "Sorry, Seb. Can't take her anywhere."

"Oh, come on," Maya chided them. "We're in the land of *amore*. What else are we gonna talk about?"

"Well…" Seb considered. "So far I've got the 'eat' part covered. Never been much for praying, being an atheist and all. And love is kind of a tall order for three weeks, so…" He swallowed back the hard knot that cinched his throat, reminding himself the point of his trip was to unwind. "I guess I'm Team Stella."

Maya whooped in triumph, but Kath shook her head.

"Oh, honey. You don't know what you're in for. She'll force more prospects on you than that old woman in *Fiddler on the Roof*."

Seb broke into a few mumbled bars of "Matchmaker, Matchmaker" in place of the mantra his therapist had assigned him as the ladies dissolved into giggles.

Two bottles of *vino rosso* and three sumptuous courses later, the laughter continued. Ceri had led them through a maze of back alleys to a picturesque square, with a small gated chapel at one end and a wood-faced trattoria at the other. Tables sprouted like toadstools in the center, corralled on three sides by ivy-woven trellises. Garlands of fairy lights competed with the glinting stars and the fat harvest moon above. Seb wouldn't have been surprised if the waiter had twirled a wand and *poofed* their dinner into existence.

He stifled a belch, scanned the detritus with a scavenger's eye. The last spoonful of the lemon soufflé beckoned him like the arms of a new lover; even sated, he still craved more. From the luscious caprese salad to the fluffy paccheri stuffed with black truffles and burrata with seafood sauce to the grilled lamb with balsamic reduction, pillowy potatoes, and garlicky rapini, their orgy of food had ridden him hard and put him away wet. As Kath ordered them a round of limoncello as a digestivo, Seb wondered how much it would be to air-lift him back to the Villa Napolitana. He said as much to the ladies.

"That's what all the stairs are for," Kath sagely explained. "Working off dinner."

Ceri scoffed. "I think we'd have to scale a few of these mountains to burn that off."

"Or…" The predatory look in Maya's eye gave Seb the heebie jeebies. "We could put Operation Stella into action. I see a few possibilities."

Only Seb's recent food intake kept him from blushing. He glanced around the square—empty except for a few elderly tourist couples and two waiters who didn't exactly scream "friends of Dorothy."

"Uh, where?"

"Wait for it."

The chapel bell tolled, a bone-quaking, eardrum-blasting sound that could have raised the dead. Or brought wolves down from the mountains. On a balcony two stories up, a husky pup howled its little lungs out. Seb would have admired the dog's "if you can't beat 'em, join 'em" attitude more if he weren't so worried he'd soon need a hearing aid. Then Andrea stepped out onto the balcony, and he almost swallowed his tongue.

Fresh from the shower, Andrea's slick wave of hair melted into a cascade of sin-black curls that matched the whorls on his bare, buff chest. He wore a pair of soccer shorts so loud they threatened to deafen the bell-husky duo, but his toned calves and peek of iliac crest looked like a second dessert. Dry-mouthed, Seb felt as if he hadn't eaten a bite.

The chapel bell tapered off with a halfhearted twang—still enough to give you an impromptu root canal—but the moonstruck husky kept on baying until a whistle from Andrea shushed him. After an ear rub and some overgenerous pets, he loped back into the apartment. His owner, however, wasn't so easily dismissed.

"Sebastiano! *Signore! Buona serra!*" Andrea leaning over the balcony rail only further stirred Seb's various appetites.

"Andrea!" his American chorus shouted, well-acquainted with Amalfi's favorite chauffeur. Not that Seb had ever set eyes on the competition.

"Come and join us for a limoncello, cher," Maya beckoned with a wink at Seb.

"Yes, Andrea, come join us!" Kath seconded.

"For you, *signore*, anything." The little husky poked his head through the curtains to see what all the fuss was about, decided people weren't interesting enough, and disappeared again. "*Un momento.*"

Which was all it took for Maya to pounce. "You didn't tell us you know Andrea."

"I don't." Seb wished he hadn't had so much wine. His face gave too much away at the best of times, but liquored up, he was practically an emoticon. "He drove me from the airport."

Kath gasped. "Are you the one who almost fainted?"

"I… no… what? It was crazy humid, and I hadn't slept in two days. I didn't faint. He just carried my backpack up the stairs."

"Ahhh." Ceri stretched the syllable into an aria. "You're the one who stiffed him on the tip."

"What? I…" Seb forced his alcohol-soaked brain to think back, then remembered he'd more or less blacked out mentally when they reached the top of the stairs. For some reason he kept returning to the image of a Jack Russell. "Shit."

"Oh, honey, he didn't mind," Kath soothed.

"You were probably too stiff yourself to think of it," Maya teased.

"No, wait. Listen, yenta—"

Andrea's arrival cut off any protest Seb might have made. A fresh, skintight green shirt fit him so snugly Seb wondered why he'd bothered, his pecs stucco-ed with wisps of chest hair. He carried a black medical bag incongruous with his football stud attire, which he plunked on the free chair instead of his—firm, delectable—ass.

"I stop only for *minuto*. My mamma, she make *baccala*."

"Just one limoncello, Andrea," Maya urged.

"You have to toast with us!" Ceri insisted.

"Think of poor Seb, stuck with us ladies all night," Kath said.

When Seb found his tongue, he clicked it. "Nonsense."

"I am happy Sebastiano is with you. When he come, he look very…" Andrea mimed *sleepy*. "How you like Amalfi?"

Seb couldn't quite keep his eyes from raking Andrea up and down before he replied, "*Bellissimo.*"

Andrea dropped his gaze, let out a bashful chuckle. The international sign for *flattered but straight*. A flare of disappointment shocked Seb out of the moment. He hadn't really thought anything would come of the ladies' efforts… had he? Was he ready for something like that? With someone who barely spoke English? He realized he hadn't thought of Henry since lunch and was suddenly stone-cold sober.

The waiter arrived with a bottle of neon-yellow liquid and five slinky flutes. He chatted in Italian with Andrea as he poured. Though Seb didn't understand a word, he suspected Andrea made sure they were treated right, a thought that warmed him. But not as much as the limoncello, of which he immediately took a generous sip. The tartness ripped down his throat and puckered his senses. Perfect.

"A toast!" Kath declared, shooting him a look for drinking without them. "Andrea, will you do the honors?"

"*Si, si.*" He appeared to give the matter serious thought. Could the future be read in the pattern of lemon rind at the bottom of a glass? Seb didn't doubt it. "To Amalfi!"

"To Amalfi!" they cheered. "*Salute!*"

"*Salute!*"

Andrea clinked each of their flutes in turn, pausing at Seb's until their gazes locked.

"You see, Sebastiano. In Amalfi, you are never alone."

The clink reverberated through Seb, vibrating his limbs, jolting his nerves, until it struck the epicenter of his heart. He drank deep of the Italian elixir, never wavering from Andrea's gray-green eyes.

Chapter Three

BLACK SAND BEACH, BAREFOOT
ON LAVA ROCK FORGED BY
THE BONES OF ANCIENTS
-#118, *IN BLUE SOLITUDES*, S. WILSON-OSAKI

Seb awoke with a surprising amount of energy the next morning for someone who had played poker into the wee hours with three ladies so ruthless they could have fleeced the most notorious card sharps of the Wild West. He'd lost all his shells and the shirt off his back when they insisted on one final round. It was the most fun he'd had in years. Not an exaggeration, and not something he wanted to look too closely at. Instead he made a mental note to pick up a seashell necklace—because he wasn't above improving his stake through a little subterfuge—and a bottle of the ladies' favorite gin so he didn't drink them dry.

After a quick breakfast of sliced peach on toast—the fruit here so ripe and sweet it didn't need any extra sugar—he set off for his first excursion out of town. Seb picked up an espresso and a *sfogliatella* from a local café Maya recommended, caffeinating as he strolled down the Via Pietro Capuano. The slender street resembled an alleyway more than a main thoroughfare, but that didn't stop cars from honking their way up and down the cobblestone street, pushing through tourists and swerving to avoid vendors' wares. Seb hummed a song from one of his favorite Disney films, *Bedknobs and Broomsticks,* as he took in the produce and products displayed in front of the stores: necklaces of dried chilies and ropes of fresh pasta, jars of homemade sauce emblazoned with family crests, skimpy knitted shawls and barely there dresses, ceramics painted in garish palettes, lemon-flavored everything. "Anything and everything a chap can unload," indeed.

Seb lingered awhile in the Piazza del Duomo, with its open-air restaurants and gelato shops, considering where they should go for dinner. He had a late-afternoon G&T pool date with the ladies, then supper at the place of his choosing. He dug out some of the cards Andrea had given him but couldn't match any to the signs. More likely Andrea had steered him toward places a bit more off the beaten track, like last night's trattoria. Seb had no quarrel with discovering the "hidden" Amalfi, vowing to do more research on his return from...

Ravello. Renowned for its concert series and as a popular wedding destination. One of the few towns on the Amalfi Coast that sits atop one of the mountains, as opposed to spilling down a ravine toward the beach, as per Henry's notes. The thought of getting into a moving vehicle that would climb the steep cliffside roads gave him flashbacks to his ride from the airport, but the bus couldn't be that bad…. could it? The few he had seen while scarfing his pizza the day before were sardine-packed with passengers. Undaunted, he trotted over to the bus stop on the far side of the marina roundabout, having learned the best way to avoid getting hit was to go about your business and let the cars avoid you. Packed though the stop was, Seb reminded himself they weren't all going to the same place, which was borne out a few minutes later when half the crowd piled into a bus for Salerno. He soon nudged his way into the last window seat on the bus for Ravello, the town Henry called "one of the most picturesque in the world."

As the bus puttered up inclines so steep skiers would be envious, Seb dug out Henry's book, reexamining the map he'd drawn and reminding himself of the places to visit. A scribbled anecdote told of a local legend: *Owner of the cameo shop says the devil took Jesus to Ravello during his second temptation to show him the beauty of the world's kingdoms.* Seb made a mental note to be on the lookout for any visiting deities.

Wedding ring sketches cluttered the last page, one of which mirrored the design of the ring Seb wore on a chain around his neck. The band of lighter skin around his left ring finger hadn't come close to fading yet; he'd only made the decision to take it off the day before his trip. He knew Henry had marriage on the brain long before his last stay here—they'd already become engaged and were considering it for their honeymoon. He imagined Henry on this same bus, on this same hill eleven years ago, thinking of him as he now thought of Henry. The circle felt complete.

Seb waited for the flood of sadness to engulf him, for the rising tide of his emotions to carve another chink in the dam of his composure. But this evidence of his husband's devotion—not that Seb needed more, given that some daydream doodle of him decorated every page of Henry's notes—comforted rather than depressed. He still felt alone even on the packed bus, still wished he could twine hands with his handsomely rumpled Henry instead of shrinking away from the sweaty tourist in the next seat. He dug the ring out of his T-shirt, slipped it back on his finger. Shut his eyes, searched for that connection his therapist promised would always be with him.

A strong but distant signal reverberated through him. Seb sat with it, in it awhile, remembering. Somehow in this place Henry had loved, it became easier to accept his reality. He kissed the ring and dropped it back into his shirt, ready to follow Henry down the path to adventure.

After shoving through the herd of tourists snapping pictures of the first thing they set eyes on upon exiting the bus, Seb made his way down a long cobblestone tunnel covered with posters of all the great musicians who'd played the Ravello Festival: Richard Wagner, Philip Glass, classical maestros, jazz pioneers, traditional operas, and fusions experiments. White stone buildings, framed as if through a telephoto lens, soon dollied into a cinematic panorama. All roads led to and from the sun-bleached expanse of the central square, flanked by a dozen umbrella-smothered cafés and dominated by the magnificent duomo.

But the real star was the view. From every balcony and patio, verdant slopes strewn with wisteria and valerian plunged toward the endless blue of the sea. On Henry's recommendation, Seb strolled the gardens of the Villa Rufolo. Through its manicured squares of begonias and thin-trunked shrub trees, craggy structures, and mossy archways, he searched for that often-imitated but nevertheless breathtaking view from the lowest tier. In the foreground a skeletal tree stretched over the twin bell towers of a humble church, its bushy upper branches fanning them with the deference shown a pharaoh. All this was set against a green strip of background coastline and always, always, dreamy blue waters. The urge to dive in was almost impossible to suppress—except when one dared look down.

Spellbound, Seb fell onto a bench and lost several hours until his stomach helpfully reminded him of things more spectacular than even the view: pizza.

One spicy sausage pie and an afternoon of hardcore shopping later—the cameo jewelry store with its craftsman owner being a highlight—Seb had bathed in enough luxury for one day. The vendors of Ravello never met an overpriced cashmere sweater or a hideous ceramic cupid they wouldn't try to hock, and fending off their predatory grins took some of the fun out of exploring the back-alley boutiques. A stroll along the Terrace of Infinity at the Villa Cimbrone helped center him, another view so inspiring that he picked up a watercolor by a local artist. But the pool, good conversation, and a lemon-slice G&T beckoned something fierce.

The buses, specifically the drivers, had other ideas. Kath had warned him the schedule was about as accurate as a sun dial at predicting their arrival time, so Seb grabbed a spot on a nearby bench—privy to yet another jaw-dropping view—and cracked open his journal. He kept an ear to the traffic as he attempted to put the indelible into words. An hour later he'd crossed out more than he'd written, a concert-sized crowd had gathered at the bus stop, and nary an engine rumble broke through their chatter. Scrambling to get in line, another thirty minutes passed as he went from lightly toasted to slow-roasted, cornered against a rock wall under the hot sun.

The blare of a horn roused the wilting crowd. A bus screeched to a halt not at the stop, but at the back of the line. A wave of passengers, who had been waiting a grand total of ten minutes, burst through the doors as soon as they opened. Seb made it within five feet before the cutoff. Those at the front of the line cursed their displeasure as the bus disappeared down the road. Reconsidering his strategy and how low the sun had sunk, he slathered on more sunscreen while letting group after group pass before him in the new-forming line.

A forty-five-minute podcast later, Seb started when another bus roared past him, halting precisely at the stop, perhaps to appease those who had been waiting nearly three hours. Like him. His "stay at the back of the line" strategy had backfired spectacularly. Seb made every crude gesture known to man at the retreating bus. He polled the English-speaking leftovers, trying to find a space among the groups sharing a cab, but the numbers never added up in his favor. Seb considered walking, then remembered all those hairpin turns and speed-demon drivers, and decided against losing a limb and/or getting sunstroke.

He collapsed onto his original bench, the view far less spectacular now he couldn't escape it. His head throbbed and his back ached. All the fluids he'd been filling himself with came back to haunt him, cramping his gut. Sweat spackled every inch of his clothing to his skin. If he ever made it back to Amalfi, he swore he wouldn't step a foot outside the city for the rest of his vacation, the other picturesque coastal towns be damned. At this point he'd blow someone if they'd get him off this mountain.

The toot-toot-toot of a chirpy horn sung out like a choir of angels. When a shadow fell over him, Seb craned his head around to see Andrea waving to him through the window of his SUV. His empty SUV. His air-conditioned SUV. Seb mentally tallied the money left in his wallet as—

"Sebastiano! You wait long? Come, come. I drive you."

With a whimper of relief that hopefully couldn't be heard over the hum of the engine, Seb grabbed his backpack, jumped over the bench, and… hesitated. Front or back? He didn't want to be presumptuous. They weren't friends, exactly. But it felt wrong, somehow, to sit in the back like some kind of lesser royalty. It was one thing when Andrea chauffeured him from the airport, but this… what was this?

Andrea shook his head, leaned over, and pushed the door to the passenger seat open. A whoosh of cool air breezed across Seb's skin, and he all but floated in. He may have emitted a postcoital-type sigh as he sank into the leather seat. After shutting the door and belting in, he lolled his head to the side to take in the sight of Andrea, sporty and fresh and lickable as a lollipop. Startling himself with that observation, Seb nevertheless had to admit it was true.

When his wandering eyes finally locked on Andrea's face, he found him suppressing a laugh.

"Thank you. Sorry about the smell."

Andrea dismissed Seb's worries with a brisk wave of his hand. "How long you wait?"

"Mmm… one hundred and sixty-three minutes."

Andrea swore in Italian.

"The buses must be good for your business."

He shrugged. "I do airport. Rich people who go Ravello-Amalfi, Amalfi-Positano, they hire a car or a driver for the week."

"Are you going to the airport now? You must have just dropped somebody off. Should I—"

"No, no. You stay. I..." For the first time in their admittedly short acquaintance, Andrea frowned. Then in perfect, lightly accented English, said, "I have a confession to make."

Seb heard his jaw crack as it fell open. "You put on that whole *paisano* routine?"

"I do. For the tourists. It..." He struggled to explain.

"Fulfills expectations?"

"Something like that. But I'm off the clock, and... I just didn't want to have to pretend with you."

Seb chuckled. "I'm honored."

"You should be. I don't give a lot of free rides." Despite the teasing, Seb didn't miss the look of relief that flickered across his face. "Do you want anything before we leave? Espresso? Gelato? Another *granita*?"

"How do you know I already had one?"

"Lucky guess."

"And I'm sure they still have them in Amalfi. Please just get me off this rock."

With a laugh, Andrea shifted the car into gear and nudged his way into the traffic. Though the road out of Ravello was bumper-to-bumper as far as Seb could see—his early escape another casualty of the bus crisis—he didn't mind that it would be a long way down.

"Bad day?" Andrea inquired once they had slammed to a halt not fifty feet from their original spot.

"Exceptional day almost ruined by transit system."

"I've had a few of those myself. Glad you weren't disappointed by Ravello."

"Is anyone ever?" Seb shifted in his seat so he could look at him directly, a view that rivaled those he'd seen that day. "What's the local perspective?"

"No complaints. It makes a lot of people a lot of money. But the families that live here all have businesses. Amalfi has a tourist section and a normal-person section. Here..."

Seb nodded. "Great place to visit, but you wouldn't want to live there."

"I don't visit." They shared a laugh, a look. Seb found himself wishing for more traffic.

"Where did you learn English?"

Andrea snorted. "From listening. This *is* a tourist town."

"True. I expected to have Google translate on standby, but everybody here understands the basics. But you're practically Shakespeare compared to some."

Another shrug. "I learned from television, travelling, university. You're right when you say most of the people here only learn enough to get by—or at least the older generation did. But, like me, sons and daughters are taking over from their fathers, and they want a stronger connection to the world."

"But tourists want old-school Italia." Seb emphasized his point with his hands in a Godfather-like gesture. "Pizza, pasta, vino, gelato. A little culture and a lot of sunshine."

Andrea laughed. "Something like that. People come here to relax. They see it as a paradise. To us it's just home."

"With the same problems it's always had."

"*Precisamente.*" He flicked a glance Seb's way, an odd little smile curving his lips. "But you didn't come here to get away, I think. You came to find something."

Seb blew out a long breath, wary of the conversation's serious turn. "I have a reason, but, to tell you the truth, I don't really know why I came here." He nudged his backpack with his foot, the weight of Henry's book against his toes a small reassurance. "I just… I had to do *something*. Staying at home in my cocoon was all I could manage for a long time. And it had to be that way. I couldn't just shrug Henry off and keep going, like…"

"No. He was your husband."

"He was my life. He was everything. And when he…" Seb inhaled a shaky breath but pushed on. No more tears. "In the blink of an eye, everything was gone. Like a sinkhole had swallowed it all up. For a long time—too long—I lay there, buried in the rubble. Waiting for the earth to quake, waiting to be sucked down. But that didn't happen. So here I am." Seb lifted his face toward the setting sun. "In paradise."

He felt a hand cover his own, squeeze tight. He turned back to find Andrea uncharacteristically solemn, starting at him as if seeing him for the first time.

"I'm glad you made it here."

Seb found his smile. "Me too."

A horn blast from the car behind broke the moment. Andrea eased away to shift the SUV into gear. The traffic now fluid, they zipped halfway down the mountain until halted by one of Italy's eternal stoplights. A curious sense of relief washed over Seb as Andrea clicked into park and turned off the engine—the better to save fuel during the ten- to fifteen-minute wait for the other direction to clear the one-lane passageway.

In the cool shadow of the hill, Seb attuned himself to the chirps of foreign birds and the buzz of foreign motors, the rustle of long leaves in stubbier trees and the shuffle of hikers' boots as they scaled the dusty off-road paths. The scent of sun-baked palms reminded him of Henry's unsuccessful attempts at making tamales, the exhaust enacting the part of their gas stove. The daydreamer in him could have basked forever in the comfortable silence that had fallen between them, could have taken back Andrea's hand and held it until the horizon smote the last glimmers of sun.

Instead he swung back into a more conversational position, propping his feet up on the armrest between the seats. "So. University?"

Andrea chuckled. "I was hoping you wouldn't catch that."

"I'm an editor. You can't get anything past me."

"Good to know. So… you run a magazine?"

"And don't try to change the subject." Hearing himself, Seb replayed that moment and thought better of his tone. "I mean, unless you want to. I didn't mean to put you on the spot. It's none of my business, really. Sorry."

"Don't apologize."

"I'm Canadian. It's a biological imperative."

Seb inwardly cheered the reemergence Andrea's dazzling smile.

"I thought you were Japanese."

"Fifty percent of my ancestors were. The other half are French. Well, French-Canadian, so from seven to ten generations removed from France. And I'm second generation on the Japanese side, so basically I'm one hundred percent Canadian."

"With hockey in your heart and maple syrup coursing through your veins."

"Yes on the maple syrup, no on the hockey. I'm not really into competitive sports."

Andrea clicked his tongue. "*Sacrilegio!*" But his eyes didn't harbor a hint of judgment. "What do you do, then, for sport?"

"Yoga, mainly. Swimming. Hiking. A bit of rock climbing, but that was more Henry's thing." Seb savored his next words, knowing how they would tantalize. "I've been known to kick a soccer ball around."

Andrea's reaction didn't disappoint, his eyes sparking and his skin glowing as if lit from within. "*Calcio?* You play?"

"Just the occasional pickup game. My sister used to play intercity."

"Ah, so it's not just syrup you have in the blood." He smacked Seb on the arm with such force it stung. "My friends and I, we play every Saturday morning. You'll be here then, yes? You should come."

"Oh, it's been a long time since I've played." Three years, give or take. Not that he'd been keeping score. "I wouldn't want to hurt your team."

Andrea waved this away with typical ease. "You won't be the worst one on the field, by far."

"How do you know? You've never even seen me play."

The corner of his sinuous lips curled up. Andrea locked eyes with Seb as if in challenge, then slowly raked his gaze down the length of him. "You'll do fine. And playing ball with a gang of sweaty Italian men is not exactly hard work." Seb swallowed hard. "You can even bring your lady friends. I'm sure they wouldn't miss it."

"Lady…" Seb couldn't pry his eyes off Andrea's plush mouth, steer his imagination away from the vision of hot, shirtless soccer players until… "Oh, crap. What time is it?"

Andrea checked his watch, a plump bicep bulging out of his slender arm, ripe as an apple. The heaviness of Seb's tongue was second only to the sudden tightness in his pants.

"18:15. Why? You missing your poker game?"

"Gin and tonics by the pool."

"Ah." Seb didn't think he imagined the disappointment that shaded Andrea's features. "Don't worry. You'll be back in time for supper."

"If not for you, I don't think I'd have gotten back at all."

Andrea,, whose hand never left his shoulder, gave it a squeeze.

"Glad to be of service, Sebastiano."

Chapter Four

DIVERGENT STAIRWAYS,
MULTICOLORED VILLAS,
ROADS TO NOWHERE
-#31, *IN BLUE SOLITUDES*, S.O. WILSON

A machine-gun knock shot Seb awake. Panic spiked his blood. He wrenched upright, slammed to the floor. Heart in his throat, starving him of breath. Head like an anvil, fever slick and hammering. *Have to get up. Have to get out.* Numb fingers clawing at his covers, cat in a bag. Everything white. Spotless. Sterile.

Had they finally had him committed?

Scrabbling, he found a hem. Beyond it something cool and smooth, like tile. Made a hole, wiggled his head out, eyes closed. Struggled till he managed a deep breath. Another. Was he imagining the smell of smoke? The *thwap* of helicopter blades? The distant drone of sirens? Swallowing back a second surge of panic, he eased open his eyes.

A white room, but no institution. Seb side-eyed the couch he had fallen off of as he sagged back into his blanket cocoon. An image came with every pound of his hangover headache: a table in the Piazza del Duomo, too many bottles of wine and limoncello, a four-piece band playing Italian classics, moonlight, dancing, Amalfi. Despite feeling like one of the sardines Chef Ottavio had scored, grilled, and smothered in lemon, he couldn't bring himself to regret it.

Another round blasted across his front door, followed by a dovelike coo.

"Coffee, get it while it's hot," Kath's muffled voice announced, followed by Maya's, "Come on, cher. You're missing all the action."

Intrigued, especially by the promise of espresso, Seb crawled out from under the blanket the ladies undoubtedly tucked him in, made sure he was decent—check, in last night's shirt and boxers—and staggered to the door. He opened it a crack—unlocked; nice one, Osaki—and reached out a hand. Espresso acquired, he took several fortifying sips before stepping outside… into Dante's Inferno.

Or former inferno. A villa three tiers above them had been reduced to a pile of rubble. Soot-smeared firemen searched the surrounding underbrush for cinders that might spark. High above, two of the neighboring peaks sent out smoke signals. The drone of approaching water planes drowned out the fading wail of sirens. All the while the pyrokinetic sun burned away any hint of cloud. On their crowded deck, another lazy day basked in the clear blue sky.

"Bushfires?" Seb plunked down on a bench beside Ceri, who blew out a ring of smoke and nodded. She apparently didn't get enough of a buzz from the charred reek of the villa's ashes. "Even over there?"

"Nah. Cigarette in a flowerpot." At his look, she barked out a laugh. "Amateurs."

"I guess we're staying in for the day." His twinge of disappointment surprised him. The whole point of a vacation was to feed your schedule to the shredder.

"Avoid the buses for sure. Roads between towns will be parking lots. But that's just common sense. Nothing beats the ferry."

Which was how he found himself on the upper level of a boat that bucketed in counterpoint to his still-aching head two hours later. Slurping from his extra-large *granita al limone*—and praying the citrus conspired with his earlier caffeine to sharpen his senses—Seb struggled to keep up with the ladies' conversation. There was simply too much view to worship.

Ever restless due to the endless stream of boats carrying tourists from town to town, the waves raced each other to shore. Villas of every size and shape, from humble stucco shacks to pillar-supported palaces adorned the voluptuous coastline. A land of peaks and valleys, of jutting promontories and of plunging ravines, strung together by lustrous amber and spackled with malachite. The fierce breeze tugged at the strands of his man bun, and volleys of spray occasionally doused his T-shirt, but Seb leaned into the wind with the eagerness of a dog out a car window. How dare Henry suggest taking the bus when there was this bliss?

"I told you," he caught Maya say. "He's gone. Between this and that card burning a hole in his pocket, we won't see him for the rest of the trip. Say your goodbyes, ladies."

"What?" Much as it pained him to tear his eyes away, he focused his attention back on the conversation. "Who's going? What card?"

Seb did not appreciate the chorus of chuckles that erupted, like an auditory pat on the head.

Ceri snorted. "I think Sleeping Beauty here has already forgotten his prince."

"I think so." Maya pouted. "And Operation Stella was going so well!"

Seb shifted his gaze from one to the other and shook his head. "I don't want to know." The chorus changed from chuckles to giggles. He swore in Quebec French under his breath.

"Language!" Kath exclaimed.

"How would you know?"

"Doesn't take a psychic," Ceri grunted.

"Just a matchmaker, apparently," Seb grumbled. He turned back to his one true love, the view, until their snickers dug so far under his skin that they drew blood. "Fine. Operation Stella. Give me a full report."

"Oh, you're not ready for that, cher." Maya smirked. "I'll start with a question. How do you suppose you got up all those stairs and onto your couch last night?"

That spooked him sober. "No. No, no, no, no, no."

"Oh, yes."

"No. Fuck." Seb buried his face in his hands, shifting his cup against his throbbing temple. Then, through his fingers, "I wasn't wearing any pants when I woke up this morning!"

"Not that," Kath broke in, shooting Maya a look. At least Seb hoped she shot Maya a look. Maya deserved the evil eye to end all evil eyes. "We were with you. He just helped you up the steps and into your apartment."

"Carried him, you mean," Ceri countered.

"*Helped*," Kath insisted.

"And left you his card," Maya continued. "He put it in your book, the one with all your notes. Said to call him if you needed another lift or help. With anything."

"The devil *was* in Ravello," Seb muttered.

"What, cher?"

"Nothing." He let out a long breath, not sure what to make of this latest turn of events. They all watched as an amphibious aircraft swooped down, scooped sea water into her hull, then soared back up to the still-smoldering mountains. "How long do you think it will take the fires to burn out?"

"Depends," Kath replied.

"On?"

"How long it stays this hot."

Seb nodded. Eventually he allowed himself a smirk.

"You ladies like soccer?"

Huffing and puffing more strenuously than the big bad wolf, Seb didn't think he could blow down a house of cards, let alone one of the seamless walls that lined the endless staircase to the Viale Pasitea. A staircase he had been climbing for going on twenty minutes, with nary a street or shop front in sight. Trash cans, locked gates, and the occasional stray cat had watched him melt from eager, determined tourist into a walking puddle of sweat and sunscreen.

He'd gone from "I can do this" to "How much farther can it be?" to "There has to be a shortcut" to amber-alert-level existential despair over the course of five hundred supersized steps, with nary a football jersey-clad driver in sight to play white knight to his simpering damsel. That reminder of how he'd once again embarrassed himself in front of Andrea—not that it mattered because he *wasn't* ready—spurred Seb on. He grunted and panted and cursed his way up and around another twist in the staircase... only to discover yet another set of steps leading to another blind curve. Behind which might be the Viale Pasitea, or the Yellow Brick Road, or the looking glass to Wonderland, or even more godforsaken steps, for all he knew. His life had become *The Staircase*, the latest from Italian horror master Dario Argento. Cue the maggots.

For the first time, Henry had steered him wrong. Seb stopped to give his screaming calves a rest, plunked his backpack and his ass on one of the fatter steps. After chugging his entire water reserve, he peeled open Henry's notebook to the page he hadn't bookmarked—an ill omen if ever there was one.

As Steinbeck famously wrote in Harper's, *'Positano bites deep. It is a dream place that isn't quite real when you are there and becomes beckoningly real after you have gone.' Here all roads lead to the Spiaggia Grande, the most popular beach on the Amalfi Coast, and the black Madonna in the church of Santa Maria Assunta, famously stolen from Byzantium. When the thieves could sail no more, they dropped their treasure, shouting, "Posa, posa!" on the first beach they came to, giving the town its name. If you, like they, land at the docks, you are faced with an impossible choice. From the Piazza Flavio Gioia, you can go right toward the church and the heavenly shopping district, or left, into the hell of the Via Pasitea, where all manner of culinary delights will tempt you.*

A simultaneous harrumph from his throat and grumble from his stomach let Henry know what Seb thought of that description. Flashing back to the dozens of seaside restaurants that greeted him as he'd hopped off the ferry, he found his second wind. Stowing the notebook, Seb clopped back down to the beach in a quarter of the time. A glass of peerless white and a trough of seafood pasta under a shady, ivy-gabled patio refueled his body and his sense of adventure. A clear view of the buff bodies tanning on endless rows of recliners on the Spiaggia Grande below encouraged him to linger. By the time a US military family's wedding party seized the table next to him—eavesdropped chatter about fighter jets was a surprising boner killer—he felt ready to tackle the stairway to heaven.

Which, thankfully, proved to be more of a path with a gentle incline. The view from the duomo almost locked Seb in for the afternoon, but the herds of tourists squeezing into an art-lined alley intrigued. The ladies correctly described Positano as higher end. Art galleries with museum-ready wares held him captive for a time until he heard the siren call of the vintners' shops and apothecaries. He picked up a bottle of artisanal citrus-flavored gin for the ladies and a '93 Mastroberardino 2003 Radici Riserva for dinner tonight.

As Seb meandered up yet another fieldstone-lined street, he came to an open ornate doorway that stole the breath from his lungs. He stared through the peak-a-boo archways at the patio of the Hotel Palazzo Murat. Dropping his bags in front of a befuddled concierge, Seb ignored his protests as he crossed the mosaic tiles into a place of dreams. For a heart-stopping moment, he thought he's stepped right into *The Talented Mr. Ripley,* one of his and Henry's favorite films and the inspiration for their anniversary trip. Seb imagined Henry as an even more suave Dickie Greenleaf, lounging on one of the blue-and-white-cushioned chaises as he waited for his awkward, endearing Tom—not Gwyneth Paltrow—to join him for a moonlit frolic.

He strolled the gardens in a daze, throat clenched and eyes stinging as he took in the cascades of purple bougainvillea, the plump lemons in the grove, the magnificent palm trees, and the eighteenth-century architecture. He'd imagined them slow dancing on their balcony under a ripe August moon more times than he could count. They had the honeymoon suite booked five years in advance. It took Seb ten tries before he successfully called to cancel. Now here he was in this magical place, and his Henry… Henry…

Seb sat on the edge of a fountain, fingers gripping into the ancient stone, willing back the tears. Knife-slit breaths scraped down his throat, the bite of the icy wind as he stood on his snowbound front porch as real to him as the sear of the late-afternoon sun. The remembered flash of police lights made him squint. The officer's life-changing words distorted to white noise as Seb's brain erupted. He crashed onto all fours on the tiled floor, gasping, whining, willing himself to be anywhere else.

Why had he come here, where every fucking molecule reminded him of the man he had lost? How could he give over to adventure when everything he did underlined the fact that Henry should be there with him? How could he hope to move on when Henry's ghost lurked around every corner? Not that he ever wanted to forget him…

When he finally managed an even breath, Seb realized a small tray had been set beside him, bearing cup of espresso, a monogrammed handkerchief, and a bougainvillea flower in a tiny glass vase. A feeling of profound gratitude overcame him, enough to urge him over to one of the patio chairs, where a deeply kind waitress moved his coffee, brought over his shopping bags, and recommended the *torta caprese*-flavored gelato.

"After sadness there is always gelato," she advised him, and Seb didn't have it in him to disagree.

The sun sank into the sea as Seb clopped down from the ferry. After he set down his gelato spoon, Seb had dug out his journal and purged his pain the only way he knew how. The gracious staff of the Palazzo Murat left him alone until they could no longer postpone dinner preparations. They shooed him off to catch the ferry without asking for a cent; Seb promised them five-star Trip Advisor ratings for their kindness. He barely flicked his eyes from the gilded waves of the Tyrrhenian Sea the entire ride back to Amalfi.

He meandered along the crowded dock in something of a fugue, his brain on autopilot as he navigated the maze of confused and overheated tourists. A horn blast from a hotel shuttle erupted beside his ear. The usual dockside madness had been amped up to eleven by the hilltop fires: two peaks still smoked, cars of all shapes and sizes jammed the coastal road, and the taxi rank resembled a used-car lot, with dozens of drivers and hundreds of passengers stranded by the traffic. Some of the more enterprising tourists had decided to walk, weaving between stalled cars and up steep inclines with no side rail to keep them from plunging to their deaths. A few tour groups of young people had taken over the bus shelter, staging an impromptu Woodstock complete with guitars, iPhone speakers, and partial nudity. A bulldog of a driver guarded the door of the only bus that hadn't made it out of the city, a salt circle of cigarettes around his feet to ward off horny couples looking for a place to get amorous.

A fight broke out among the taxi drivers just as Seb reached for his journal to capture the scene. No fisticuffs, but one could be forgiven for thinking a few punches had landed given the men's beet-red faces and aggressive gestures. They wielded their hands, teeth, and spit like broadswords and battleaxes, their insults volcanic arias of bile. Seb expected the other drivers to place bets on this cockfight, circling them to get close enough to catch a flying feather or two. Instead they shuffled around their cars, kept their distance.

It was only as he smacked down a vulgar gesture and stomped away that Seb recognized Andrea. His sparring partner shouted a few impotent insults after him, but Andrea had already deployed his cell, recounting the incident in rapid-fire Italian to a sympathetic ear. Seb watched him circle behind the other cabs, pacing out his frustration.

Andrea hopped onto one of the anchor-shaped rocks that lined the docks, anger stringing his trim physique tight as a bow. Another day, another football jersey. Today the green of the US Avellino Wolves. Andrea certainly looked predatory as he surveyed the marina.

Before Seb could stop himself, he set out at a cautious pace toward him. Something about his lone wolf stance, abject but defiant, lured him forward. Andrea might lash out, but this was a man who'd seen Seb at his most vulnerable and responded with kindness. Had come to his rescue almost every day of his trip. The least Seb could do was return the favor.

"Turf war?" Seb climbed up on the rock as Andrea jammed his thumb down on his phone and cursed under his breath. "Are you a Shark or a Jet?"

Andrea scoffed, reached out his hand to help him up. Aftershocks of fury still vibrated through it. When Seb held on a second too long, Andrea pulled away, clicked his tongue.

"Not here."

"Was it that kind of argument?"

Andrea sighed. "Maybe."

"Do you want me to go?"

"No. Absolutely not. You're the only not-crazy person I've spoken to all day."

Seb laughed. "I don't know about that..." This earned him a smirk. He felt ridiculously accomplished. "I'm guessing today has been a total wash?"

"Could have been worse." Andrea shrugged. "It's not the first time this..." He waved an exasperated hand up at the chaos. "I plan for it. Called in favors. Only lost two fares, which is not too bad. Or three, now, because of that *testa di cazzo*."

"Do I want to know what that means?"

Another smirk. "Under different circumstances... maybe."

"Now I'm really curious."

In the corner of his eye, he saw Andrea cant toward him but resisted the urge to match his stare.

"Are you?"

Seb let the moment hang a few beats too long, feeling as if he dangled from the edge of a cliff. Would he find the strength to pull up and over, or should he just let himself fall? Still weary from his emotional afternoon, he decided to get a leg up.

"Of course. I'm a translator."

"Is that what they're calling it these days?"

Seb let out a belly laugh that must have confused the hell out of the other driver. He clapped Andrea on the shoulder—bigoted colleagues be damned—and gave it a squeeze.

"Let's get a drink. Or, better yet, let me buy you dinner. I'm told I have a reputation to salvage, in more ways than one. Unless you have somewhere to be..."

Andrea grunted, pointed to his SUV stuck behind three lines of parked taxis and shuttles. "Not tonight. But don't you have gin and tonics by the pool?"

"Ladies are in Capri. Expected back late." Seb caught a glint of that high-voltage smile.

"Then I have you all to myself?"

"Seems like."

Their eyes met, and Seb skipped a breath, overwhelmed and a little intimidated by the heat that simmered there. But he was here for adventure, and what better kind than the invitation in Andrea's gray-green eyes?

"Then lead on, Sebastiano."

Despite the cool breeze sweeping in from the sea in the sun's wake, Seb's back felt scorched by the full force of that fiery orb with Andrea's heat radiating behind him as he wove through the crowd. Percussionists with makeshift drums and kitted-out tablets took over from the folk guitars under the bus shelter, underscoring Seb's excitement and nerves as they darted through traffic. The sense of playing hooky—not just Andrea from work, but Seb from the realities of his life these last solitary years—loosed one of the binds around his heart.

As they emerged from the tight alleyway into the Piazza dei Dogi, Seb realized he hadn't thought this through. Restaurants sprouted like dandelions in Amalfi, but only a few were worthy of being plucked for your salad. Turning away from the avid gazes of a dozen maître d's in the table-strewn piazza, he caught his shrub-headed companion's bemused look.

"I'm starting to feel like a blind man leading a seeing-eye dog. Where do you want to go?"

His typical Italian noncommittal shrug didn't impress. "Wherever you like."

Seb scrutinized his face, looking for a sign. "You've never eaten at any of these places, have you, man of a thousand business cards?"

Andrea laughed. "You try explaining to your mamma that you had dinner somewhere else when you were in town."

"Point taken. And we can't go anywhere else…"

"That depends on how tired you are."

Seb considered this awhile. "I'd manage a second wind if we stopped for a *granita*."

"I've created a monster." Andrea chuckled, turning against the tide of tourists streaming in from the marina. After working his way through the crowd a few steps, he reached back to urge Seb to fall in close beside him, a wrinkle of uncertainty creasing his brow. Diving in with both, er, hands, Seb clamped a hold on his shoulders, half steering him, half being tugged down the short alley to his favorite café. The flow of bodies forced him so close he could smell Andrea's citrusy cologne, the tantalizing olive-skinned nape of his neck peek-a-booing through the sweat-loosened waves of his hair. Though Seb resisted the desire to nest his face in his curls, nibble on that pale patch of neck the sun missed, he acknowledged how long it had been since he'd felt something, anything, for a man not named Henry Wilson.

Once armed with matching cups and away from the crowds, they followed the car-jammed coastal road up a twisty hill toward the Hotel Luna Convento, a converted monastery perched on a cliffside. Seb found walking inches from a dead drop onto a shoreline of toothsome rocks with only a flimsy rail between you and oblivion much easier with Andrea in front of him. He drank contentedly as Andrea chatted with local drivers they passed, relishing the tart pinch of lemony ice melting on his tongue.

They rounded the bend, veering away from the hotel

restaurant with its enticing bar and exceptional seaside view. The road expanded, and Andrea fell in at his side, smile only slightly puckered by the *granita*. A brolike shoulder shove had Seb wondering if he'd misread the entire situation but also got his Spidey-senses tingling.

"So what was going on back there? Is he your competition?"

Andrea snorted. "My cousin Bruno. He's... I'm not sure how you would say it in English. *Scansafatica.* Has a lot of opinions about everybody but himself. Hates the tourists, hates the government, hates everybody but his mamma and his car. He can't keep a job. It's his mouth, his attitude. But he's family, so..." Another shrug.

"He helps you out?"

"That's what he would say."

"And you?"

Andrea sighed. "I use him only in emergencies, or when I can't listen to my *Zia* Fabiana yell at him anymore. There have been problems with the clients. Sometimes it's easier to lose a fare."

"But that must mean losing clients."

"Sometimes yes. So I try not to call him more than one day a week, but with yesterday, and now..." He waved at the traffic. "But he took his time, stopped to talk to this girl he's chasing, and we lost the fare anyway. Very important client. One of our regulars who tips well. Travels here often. But the client knows about the fires and the traffic, so this time he decided to stay in Sorrento for the night, and I arranged something with another friend to take him there. It worked out."

"Still a lot of trouble for nothing."

"Precisamente. So I refused to pay my cousin today. This is not the first time he does this. And I can't afford to lose any more business. There is, as you say, competition. But."

"But?"

Andrea inhaled deeply, looked out to sea. "He knows things. About me. Things that… Here, it's not like in Canada."

"Things that your family doesn't know?"

"No, no. My mamma, my sisters, they love me. But other drivers… It's very macho. You can't advertise."

"They see it as a weakness."

Andrea nodded. "Another headache I don't need."

"And I'm guessing your cousin doesn't let anyone forget it."

"Only thing he does remember about me. And likes to shout about. Loudly. In public." Andrea slowed his pace as they approached a tunnel. The pedestrian path veered away from the road, through another cliffside terrace. Mindful of the crowded tables, Andrea waited until they hit the long staircase down to the beach to continue. At least these steps went down. "I'm not in the closet. Most people who know me know—"

"I get it," Seb reassured him. "Even in Canada, I wouldn't want someone screaming about my personal life to the wrong audience."

"*Si*. Here, there are still hate crimes. Or people will shut you out. Not recommend you to their customers or their friends."

"Deadly in your business. 'You scratch my back, I scratch yours' is pretty much the way of life here."

"You've been paying attention."

Seb attempted a version of the Italian shrug. "I try." He stopped on a landing to admire the castle-like city of Atrani, a tessellated series of villas that fanned out from a central square, guarded by an ancient roadway pierced by stone arches through which the beach spilled out. Seb felt like he should be dressed in Don Quixote's medieval armor, not sandals and cargo shorts. "You'd think he'd be more discreet about the personal life of the only man in town who'll give him a job."

"It also probably wasn't a good idea to sleep with his ex-girlfriend."

Seb choked on his *granita*, fighting to control his shock and his laughter. Andrea patted him on the back till he could breathe again. And laugh some more.

"I'm sensing there's a story here."

"Only that I like to make things harder for myself."

"Understatement."

Andrea fell quiet for a moment, to the point that Seb feared he'd offended him. After several awkward moments, Andrea drew in a long breath, then declared, "I'm bisexual."

Seb smiled, nodded encouragingly. When nothing came after, he prompted, "That must be hard. Especially if people have—"

"Expectations. Yes. When I was young, I didn't really understand the gay side of myself. Didn't want to understand it. So I went with girls. But then when I was away at university…"

"The other shoe dropped. And now you get a lot of, 'But if you like women…' Or in your cousin's case, 'If you like men, stay away from my ex.'"

Andrea frowned. "You've heard the gossip?"

"Me? No, no. I've just heard this story before. Most bi people get some version of that."

"Are you…?"

"More in theory than in practice. I think most queer people dated the opposite sex in high school, or tried to, to avoid rocking the boat. But I wasn't fooling anyone, especially my girlfriends. One of them actually bought me a bottle of lube and a box of condoms for my birthday, and begged me to take her dancing in the Gay Village. Wasn't thrilled when she had to find her own way home."

Andrea laughed, too weak for Seb's liking. "Sounds like my sister."

"You're lucky there. Mine married a caveman who keeps pushing her to send me to a mental institution for reconditioning. Thinks now that Henry's out of the picture, I have a shot at a 'real' relationship."

A curse that required no translation spat off Andrea's tongue. Remembering that he was trying to calm him down, not rile him up again, Seb made a second attempt at a shrug and gestured toward the beach.

"This conversation is getting too serious to be had on an empty stomach. My last carb infusion was a whole six hours ago. I need some starch, stat. These staircases aren't going to climb themselves."

Seb took the soft chuckle that sad attempt at a joke earned, liked better the gentle push to the small of his back as they made their way to the beach. They scored a seaside table at a little shack of a restaurant under one of the archways. With its makeshift canopy bordered by potted palms, the atmosphere felt more surf bum than serf. Seb glanced at the menu but left the ordering to Andrea, only consulting on pizza toppings—spicy sausage—and color of wine—red, of course.

Instead Seb reclined back in his chair and looked, really looked, at the man across the table. Stripped of his fake accent, his taxi driver hospitality, his natural caregiver's need to please, he appeared vulnerable. Gentle in a way his handsomeness masked to those who only saw surfaces. Seb's hand twitched, the impulse to reach across the table and take Andrea's hand a strong one. But that would be an invitation Seb wasn't sure he was ready to send. Here in the moment, on a stage, Seb's wants held court. Later, in more intimate surroundings, they might prove as transparent as the emperor's new clothes.

"So. Your cousin's ex. What's the story there?"

Andrea groaned, bent his head to hide a smile just this side of wolfish. "You don't want to know."

"Oh, I definitely want to know. Don't make me ask the gossips."

Finally a fulsome laugh. "There's nothing to tell. They were together when they were teenagers. He hadn't even seen her for two years. She lives in Maiori. I was there one night, after *calcio.* I belong to a club. We went to a bar after our game. She was there." He threw up his hands. "Same old story. Boring."

"You left out the part where you did it for revenge." Seb

didn't know what he found more delicious, the halfhearted shake of Andrea's head or the blush that tinted his cheeks. "I think you're a better storyteller than that."

A theatrical sigh. "How did you know?"

"I'm a writer. I know."

"I thought you were an editor. Though I confess I don't really know what that means."

"Never heard that one before," Seb quipped as the waiter set down an orgy of fresh seafood between them. He salivated over the gorgeous platter of langoustines, shrimp, clams, mussels, and calamari, eyeing their succulent flesh like he would a new lover's spread thighs. His libido might not survive such indulgence with Andrea's bright eyes glinting at him all the while. Seb dove in before he could think too much about it. "I edit and translate for work," he elaborated between mouthfuls. "I write for myself."

"Have you published any books?"

"In the past. But that wasn't even me. I've done translations of classic Japanese haiku. Cliché, I know…" He quaffed down a particularly briny clam, savoring its salty bite. "Writing is more like my therapy now. I purge and prune. The writer spews it all out; the editor cleans it all up. But I'm too much of a perfectionist to send it out into the world."

"Might be good for you to let it go."

Seb smirked. "You don't say?"

Andrea's laugh echoed through the archways and out to sea, and Seb found himself that much more enchanted with the man of uncharted depths. He gave over to the food, the wine, the conversation, the starry night, the turrets looming above, and the grit of sand beneath their feet as they strolled back to Amalfi, tipsy and content.

Seb didn't feel one pinch of ache in his arches until they came to the vaultlike doors of the Villa Napolitana and he faced the prospect of that endless staircase. And what it would mean to have an escort for the second night in a row.

He leaned back against a wall that had seen entire civilizations rise and fall, basking in the sight of Andrea, whose blood simmered with the lusts of the ancients, who smoldered with discomfiting allure. Eyes like silver dollars on a moonlit beach. Streetlamps crowning the waves of his dark hair like the head of the Virgin. He knew the man within to be kind, playful, honorable, and Bacchus knew Seb had tested his patience. Did he dare disturb the universe? In a minute, was there time for decisions and revisions another minute would reverse?

"'Sebastiano and the Staircase.'" Andrea chuckled, closed just enough of the space between them so Seb didn't bolt. "I could write that poem. Or perhaps a play in the commedia dell'arte style."

"Dirty limerick."

"Ah. Just so."

"Was it bad last night? I don't want to know what happened almost as much as I want to know."

"Bah." Andrea waved the thought away. "It was nothing. Too much dancing."

"Too much wine."

"Limoncello," Andrea corrected.

"Ah. The critical error."

That shrug again. "You'll know for next time."

"But did I…"

"Did you…?"

"Did we…" Throat parched but tongue heavy, Seb forced himself to meet that numinous gaze.

"Sebastiano…" Andrea stroked a tender touch down the side of his face, over his lips. "I do not go where I am not invited. And you were in no state last night to entertain guests. But tonight…" The second stroke lingered on the arch of his cheek, the hollow beneath, at the edge of a mouth Seb couldn't bring himself to open to him. "I want nothing more than to make that climb with you. But I think… I feel you are not ready."

He dropped his hand to Seb's chest, pressing it over the space where his heart would be if it weren't in his throat, choking him.

"I want to be," he rasped, hating and clinging to every word.

"*Sì*. And you will be. You have come here to shed your skin, and if I have helped with that… I am glad. It's been a beautiful night."

"I'll never forget it."

Seb stared in disbelief as Andrea broke into one of his dazzling smiles. "Nor will I." He pressed a soft kiss to Seb's forehead—a benediction—then slowly pulled away.

"Will I see you again?"

"Of course. This is Amalfi." Andrea threw his arms wide as he hopped off the sidewalk into the street. "*Calcio*. Saturday. The *campo* by the marina. Don't forget to bring us some cheerleaders."

"Only if I can be one of them."

"Then you'd better wear a skirt."

"I'll see what I can do." Seb forced a smile as Andrea neared the bend in the road, not ready for him to go but with nothing to offer him should he stay. "It has been a beautiful night," he called after him.

"*Sogni d'oro*, Sebastiano."

Chapter Five

SOMNAMBULANT NIGHT;
SHADOWS AND SECRETS SLITHER
THROUGH WILD LEMON GROVES
-#87, *IN BLUE SOLITUDES*, S. WILSON-OSAKI

Seb plucked out a lonely tune on the plastic bands of the lounge chair as he stared up at a starless sky. The small copse of fig trees at the far end of the pool didn't shade sun worshippers much during the day. At night they took on an otherworldly aspect, a circle of spindly ents whose poky, skipping movements stole away your sadness. Seb hummed and strummed a Quebecois folk song, hoping to entice them, but he couldn't feel a tingle of their magic.

A second, richer voice chimed in. Maya, nightdress and braids by Cleopatra's handmaids, shoved his legs aside to make room for her imperial majesty. She gave his thigh a squeeze and continued to sing, morphing the song into a gorgeous Creole hymnal as far away from Quebec's winter landscape as the moon was from the sun. Seb shifted to his side to give her more room, propped his head on his arm to listen to his nightingale. Just what his sleepless night had been missing.

When at last her song died out on a note as full and regal as the lady herself, Seb embraced the silence. Maya, the glow of the streetlamps gilding the edges of her face, pressed his free hand between her own, waiting him out. Still unable to trace the map of his failure, Seb diverted.

"Now how does a girl from New Orleans know the words to Gilles Vigneault?"

"She doesn't. But she's a big fan of Rufus Wainwright."

Seb chuckled. "So am I. Henry…" He scowled.

"Talk about him if you need to, cher."

"But I shouldn't. Not as much as I do."

"Nonsense. Whoever told you moving on means forgetting the most important part of your life doesn't know much about living."

"Neither do I, lately."

"You're here, aren't you? You're trying. And don't quote me that *Star Wars* garbage. There is such thing as trying." Seb barked out a laugh, shocked. "Don't give me that look! Twelve-year-old boys are not the only ones who worship Han Solo."

"Han Solo or Harrison Ford?"

"I don't see why I have to choose."

A reluctant smile crept over his face. "Well, General Maya Organa—"

"That has a nice ring to it."

"In this galaxy, Operation Stella self-destructed."

"Aww, cher." She tightened her grip with one hand, stroked the back of his with the other. "What have I told you about absolutes?"

"What do you mean?"

"If it doesn't work out with your knight in shining SUV, try again with someone else. Operation Stella is about you getting your groove back. It doesn't matter with who." His expression mustn't have been too convincing because Maya sighed, then gave his knuckles a smack. "Tell me what happened."

Seb gave her the Encyclopedia Britannica version, from his Positano meltdown to the scuffle at the marina to their beachside dinner and stroll with a side of rejection. Even Seb couldn't believe all those events had occurred in one day and had to agree when Maya exclaimed…

"Well, no wonder you weren't up for it. You'd already tied yourself in more knots than you need for a merit badge."

"That's kind of my natural state of being."

"Don't think I hadn't noticed." For a long time, she stared into the shimmery waters of the pool, as if some divine, Busby Berkeley-type siren would burst out with the perfect solution amidst billows of foam and spray. "All right, time to get serious. Before you met your husband, were you a Matt or a Ben?"

"Er… pretty sure I've always been a Sébastien."

She clicked her tongue. "Don't be smart. Were you more of a one-man-at-a-time guy like Matt Damon, or a love 'em and leave 'em like—"

"Ben Affleck." Seb laughed. "I think the gay version would be a Brian or a Michael."

"Oh, from *Queer As Folk*? That's much better. And so is the British version."

"Agreed. I just assumed—"

"It's all right, cher. I would have too." Maya dragged over another lounger and propped her feet up. "So?"

"Michael, of course."

She dismissed his self-flagellation with a brisk gesture. "The love of a good man can change a lot of wicked ways. But then your brand of loyalty can't really be taught. And trust me, I would know." Her smile eased something in him he hadn't realized had been aching. "You need to ask yourself: Do you want this trip to be the final step in your recovery, or your first chance to move on? Don't answer right away."

Seb nodded.

"Next, what does moving on mean to you right now? Does it mean a little flirtation, a lot of fun, and the companionship of a very friendly someone? Or does it mean going full Stella? And remember, cher, there is no wrong answer. There is only the answer that is wrong for you right now."

Seb gave her words the consideration they deserved, so much that when Ceri peeked through the entranceway, wiggled a bottle in their direction, and pointed to the upstairs patio, he almost didn't notice. But he did catch her slouch-and-lean as she said goodbye to Lucia, who stopped on the landing to check out the pool, and possibly Ceri.

Maya nudged him with her knee.

"Therapist, social worker, or school counselor?"

"Foster parent. Twenty years. And a nurse for a decade. Now I'm the social coordinator at our local library, and I couldn't be happier."

"So you're saying I'm no better than a delinquent teenager?"

Maya gave him one of the best stink eyes he'd ever witnessed. "I'm *saying* I know heartache. And there is another side. But you got to grab for it with both hands."

Seb reached out and seized hers, grateful that, if nothing else, he'd found a lifelong friend in this fabulous lady.

"Those are some lucky kids."

"Huh! I'll tell them you said so, next time they come begging." She shook her head. "Never even wanted to be a mother, and somehow I ended up with six damn squawking chicks."

"At the same time?"

"Over the years. Still have one waiting for me back home. Saved the hardest for last, of course."

"That's what vacations are for."

"You don't need to tell me." She eased up onto her feet, then offered him a hand. "Come on, cher. If you're not sleeping, might as well be drinking with us."

"Truer words, truer words."

Seb took a long last look at his enchanted circle, saw the little forest for the trees. Maya's words and wisdom had sunk deep, and as he followed her toward the staircase, he felt a metamorphosis stirring within.

Nothing in his life thus far had prepared Seb for waking up in bed with a woman. Fortunately Kath didn't snore. Fully clothed and lying atop the comforter, Seb snuck back to his apartment before she could spoon him in her sleep, fairly certain his virtue was intact. Catching a glance at himself in the bathroom mirror as his shower heated up, the sun-kissed, tousled-haired merman who gazed back startled him. Neck and arms garlanded with seashell jewelry and torso taut with almost-defined muscle, his scaly blue towel disappeared anything below his waist. If you cut him in jade and sold him as a souvenir, he might even tempt a few tourists.

He smiled at himself, channeling a little Narcissus, but for a good cause: self-esteem.

A shower and a change later—his clothes from the day before possibly needing to be burnt after all that stair-climbing—he decided to play mum to the ladies who had been so welcoming to him. He set the coffee maker to grinding them up some espresso, heaped three plates with pastries, toast, and fruit, not forgetting a few packets of Splenda for Kath. He added a bowl of decorative lemons—this was Amalfi, after all—but decided against any hair of the dog. They'd all be into the G&Ts soon enough.

Checking the clock, Seb realized it was a bit too early to play rooster. He puttered around his apartment for a while, finally settling in when he came across Henry's notebook. He flipped through the pages upon pages of recommendations, but nothing drew the eye.

Not today, when the sunlight dappling the aquamarine tiles seemed so much livelier than before. Not this particular morning, when a bite of strawberry was berrier than ever. Not here, in this place, where he had come to memorialize and to move on. *The time has come,* Seb's libido said, *to talk of shiny things. Of sculpted locks and ass and calves; of gray-green-colored rings.*

Seb clicked open the apartment safe and slid the notebook inside. After a moment's consideration, he slipped the chain that held his wedding ring from around his neck and laid it over the notebook. Today, he decided, was all him.

Which was how he found himself, four hours later, seaside at a five-star hotel. Owned by the same firm as the Villa Napolitana, Seb and the ladies had purchased a day pass for the pool and spa facilities at a discounted rate. Still, the Hotel Santa Caterina was possibly the least Henry-approved environment on the coast. Seb flicked thoughts of his husband's disdain out of his mind—not hard when being served by a fleet of deep-tanned and short-shorted waiters who kept your side table jammed with bowls of fresh fruit, nuts, and chips as you worshipped the sun.

Spoilt for choice in the swimming department, Seb had tried the saltwater pool and the sea, which could be reached from a diving platform a few steps below their ivy-pillared lounge area. A glass elevator scaled the rock face behind them up to the hotel proper, where another lavish terrace and dining area with even more lavish prices awaited them. This was a place where guests couldn't even spell the word "no."

Just because she could, Ceri bid the waiters bring their lunch to the fleet of lounge chairs they'd commandeered. Feeling as sun drunk as a pirate king, Seb watched them spin quenelles of lemon cream pasta into bowls at the bar while he picked at his caprese salad. The unlimited free refill bar.

"Good?" Kath asked.

"*Molto bene.*" Seb grinned, feeling light as a cloud. "How did you find out about this place?"

"You haven't been getting the flyers?" Ceri stubbed out a Gauloise to start on her lunch.

"Lucia mentions it every time we've called her," Kath added. "I'm surprised she doesn't make her little dog wear an ad board."

Ceri gawked at her sister. "That's a very me thing to say."

"If it's true, it's true. This is a lovely place, but even for a discounted day pass, it's not cheap. It's not fair to rub it in people's noses if they're on a budget."

"So worth it, though," Seb chimed in with his mouth full, to which Maya added an "Amen."

"Manners, hon," Kath mommed him. But everybody laughed when he gave her the finger.

"Henry would have agreed," Seb remarked, taking his ability to talk about him without the emotional crash and burn for a test drive. "He was all about affordable travel. Even gave talks about it to inner-city parents, organized field trips for underprivileged schools, and stuff like that. 'Seeing the world is the best education there is.'"

"He was a keeper," Ceri said. "And you're here because…"

"This is *my* vacation. Even if it took me a while to figure that out. And—" Seb opened his arms to their surroundings, endless sea, soaring cliffs, hot waiters, and all. "—can you imagine if I'd missed out on this?"

"Cheers to that!" Kath toasted, and the four of them clinked glasses.

An hour later, having devoured half of one of Kath's historical romances and deepened his tan, Seb heeded the call of the sea. Armed with a pipe-cleaner-like flotation device that he could hook under his shoulders, he charged off the diving platform and into the strong current. The push-pull of the waves from passing ferries and motor boats turned a simple swim to the outer buoy into a white-water rafting-esque thrill ride. Seb stabbed into the waves with each powerful stroke, kicked out against the undertow. No swimming pool propelled you up to body surf with your chest or splashed over your head while you tread water. Seb slammed his palm into the buoy as if hitting the buzzer in an Olympic trial, marveled at how far out he'd swum when he looked back at the shore.

Reclining back into his DayGlo pipe cleaner "chair," Seb gave over to the mercy of the current. It took its time drifting him back to the diving platform. He watched ships small and large ferry tourists up and down the coast, trying not to think about what those boats might be dumping into the magnificent sea. He basked in this moment that was wholly his, in this most perfect union of sun, sea, and sky.

Salt on his lips reminding him of what might have been the night before, his woozy mind conjured an image of Andrea floating beside him, hair slick and black as seal skin; thick, wet lashes like smiles under his half-mast eyes; sinuous body disappearing into a pair of tight gym shorts, barely visible beneath the sun-sparkled waves.

Seb laughed out loud at the soft-core stylings of his imagination. Canting into the current, he let the waves lap at him with their silky tongues. Let Poseidon's nereids surge and swell around him. Let the pleasures of the day bubble up within until he thought he might pop.

Dragging himself out by the ladder, Seb felt a little giddy and a lot drowsy. The warm spray of the shower mellowed him. He suppressed the urge to pinch the asses of the pair of hot waiters who escorted him over to his lounge chair, where a refill of his spiked *granita al limone* awaited him like a toast from Poseidon himself.

Chapter Six

TUFTS OF SCORCHED SHRUBS
DOT THE ROLLING AMBER HILLS,
GOATS FROLIC AND GRAZE
-#171, *In Blue Solitudes*, S. Wilson-Osaki

Cracking off a strand of filo from his *sfogliatella* late the next afternoon, Seb relaxed into the relative tranquility of the Piazza Duomo. The liquorice-striped, mostly Romanesque church was like a giant gingerbread house with breadcrumbs leading away from, not to, its limited pleasures. Seb admired the artistry and history of the building, which did little to inspire religious fervor. The espresso sold by the humble cafés gathered around the square, however…

He dug out an orange-and-cinnamon-laced dollop of warm ricotta, smeared it on his tongue. Closing his eyes as he savored the unctuous filling, he forced himself to ignore the pesky voice of Old Seb nattering in his ear, scolding him for not heading down to the marina to catch the ferry to Capri that morning.

Not that he didn't want to go to Capri. But New Seb, dedicated to nothing more than enjoying his snack, hesitated over following any plan that hewed too close to the notebook. New Seb wanted to let the day unfold, led by only his curiosity and desires. New Seb had spent more time getting reacquainted with his dick than writing in his journal once the ladies had turned in the night before. New Seb suspected if he sat still long enough, he just might get his groove back.

Something tickled at his ankle, curled around his calf. A pair of jewel-green eyes blinked lazily up between the folds of his sarong. (New Seb flouted traditional gender roles and wore what he felt most comfortable in.)

"*Piccolo* Andrea!" The cat gave his pastry-scented hand a sniff, then rubbed its fuzzy head against his knuckles. He scooped the little gray tabby up into his arms, petting and cooing until feline Andrea was a puddle of purr. *If only the man himself were this easy to please.*

A car horn trumpeted. Claws bit deep. With a wriggle and a yowl, Little Andrea shot off up the road. Seb considered following him—because why not?—until a familiar voice sung out from the window of the SUV suddenly stopped in front of his table.

"Sebastiano!"

As wide and alluring as ever, human Andrea's smile prompted Seb to abandon half his *sfogliatella* for that face in the window. Not impressed with how bashful he felt, New Seb performed his best car lean, letting his loose V-neck T-shirt fall open to reveal his tanned, if slender, chest. He almost stumbled over his own feet when he got a glimpse of Andrea, shower-fresh in a crisp black shirt and tight jeans, with nary a team jersey or soccer short in sight. The man rocked the 'Roman businessman on holiday' look better than his clients. Of which, curiously, there were none.

New Seb, fighting through his shyness, wolf-whistled.

"Where are you off to, looking…" He couldn't quite bring himself to say any of the words that came to mind out loud.

Andrea opened his mouth but seemed to mentally cross out several answers before he asked, "Would you like to come?"

Seb didn't hold back a single inch of the grin that stretched his mouth.

"I would, yeah." He grabbed his backpack, espresso, and pastry, then paused. "Are we going far? Do we need refreshments? Have you eaten?"

"I did. And we need to hurry. But they'll have everything we need there."

Seb almost bounced into the front seat. "And you're not going to tell me where that is, are you?"

Andrea laughed. "Maybe in a little while."

"Once we're out of the city? No turning back?"

"You make it sound sinister." The light changed, and they were off. "Maybe I just want you to myself for a little while."

The back of Andrea's hand grazed Seb's as he reached for the stick, mirroring the caress of his tiny namesake.

"I've got no problem with that," New Seb declared and settled in for the ride.

They followed the coastal road farther east than Seb had ever been, past the inland turn for Ravello and smaller towns like Maori and Cetara until they reached the outskirts of Salerno. Typically spellbound by the scenery, Seb fell into a kind of trance despite the hairpin swerves and steep turns. Andrea gave him free rein over his iPod, so Seb spent a good twenty minutes investigating his taste in music—indie rock, eighties electronica, classic film soundtracks, and twenties jazz standards. He approved. He teased Andrea by putting on Ennio Morricone's greatest hits, specifically the theme to *The Good, The Bad, and The Ugly,* but settled on the latest Radiohead. Somehow the alien sounds provided the perfect counterpoint to the sun-baked splendor of the view.

They chatted a bit at stoplights, but something about the road lulled them into a cozy, companionable silence. Though his list of questions about Andrea had only gotten longer since getting in the SUV, they evaporated from Seb's mind whenever he turned to contemplate Andrea himself, a study in alert relaxation in the driver's seat. His posture differed from that first drive from the airport, more casual, and yet… Something buzzed around him, a force field of tension that intrigued Seb even as it warned him off. Andrea expected, perhaps, that Seb would voice his questions, dig into his secrets now that they were down the rabbit hole together—and Old Seb, he had to admit, would have pulled out all his carrots by now.

But patience often yielded, and so as they sped onto the A3 highway toward the Cilento National Park, or so Seb guessed, he let the mood, music, and magnificence feed his poet's soul. The craggy peaks of the Amalfi coast gave way to rolling, shrub-speckled hills ringed with orchards. Farmhouses poked through the foliage, two-storey white or yellow buildings with sandpaper roofs and fieldstone staircases, tinder-stick gables sheltering the paths to and from the barn. The occasional pool winked at him, aquamarine eyes amidst amber soil and umber dust.

"*Agriturismo*," Seb remarked. "I almost did one of these."

"For your whole trip?" Andrea made a noise in the back of his throat.

"No, only a few days. Just to see another side of Italy. And the quiet was appealing."

"Quiet Amalfi is not."

Seb chuckled. "No. Especially when you're dancing in the street till two a.m."

He caught a glimpse of Andrea's smirk, but then that handsome face sobered into an expression more befitting the bust of an ancient philosopher. The force field had almost become palpable, waves of tension emanating off him like a scorched stretch of desert highway.

"I haven't…" Andrea cursed as someone cut him off. "You need to know, before we…" He opened and shut his hands a few times, but even that inbred orchestration failed him.

"Whatever it is, it's okay." When this was met with silence, Seb added, "Maybe I'm not the only one who isn't ready."

A bitter laugh escaped Andrea's throat. "You're not wrong."

"Okay. So where do we go from here?"

Andrea sighed. "That depends. I've avoided sharing

something with you. I... I'm not even sure why."

"Omission as opposed to commission?"

"Something like that." He still wouldn't meet Seb's eyes. "I'm making too much of it. You're probably gonna laugh. At least I hope you're gonna laugh."

"God, what the hell is it? Now you have to tell me."

"Right. I know. Fuck." Finally their gazes locked. "I'm a veterinarian."

The words hung in the air for heartbeat after heartbeat until Seb did, indeed, burst out laughing.

"That's it? Your big secret? All applicants must love dogs?"

"I... What?" Thankfully Andrea coughed out a few chuckles of his own. "What are you talking about?"

"I was beginning to wonder, is all. Not about you, but... well. Impromptu trip to a remote location with a charming guy I got to know very quickly, who gets more and more tense the closer we get to God knows where... Don't tell me you've never read an airport thriller."

"Oh, Sebastiano..." Andrea doubled over, cackling. He grabbed Seb's hand and kissed deep into his palm, the tension flooding out of him in waves that rivaled the Tyrrhenian sea. "Your imagination is a thing of beauty."

"Gets me into more trouble than it keeps me out of." He let Andrea twine their fingers, but not off the hook. "So. University. That's one mystery solved."

"Yes."

"You graduated?"

"Yes."

Seb watched him, wondering how hard to push. Wanting to push very hard indeed, his curiosity turned the butterflies in his stomach into wasps. "Should I ask the obvious question, or should I just let it be?"

Andrea's look just then, of gratitude, of admiration, of fondness, was answer enough.

"I was in the second year of my residence when my papa got sick. He came to the city to get treatment. I juggled both, so I was able to finish while I helped him. But when it got to the point where… Well, he wanted to be home, and it was easier for my mamma and my sister. So I took a… I'm not sure what you call it. I left for a while. And while I was here, I worked for him. He didn't want all his work to be for nothing. And once he was gone… My mamma, I couldn't leave her. So I stayed. And she got better."

"And still you stayed."

He nodded. "There aren't that many clinics in Amalfi. Family businesses that don't have money for anyone else. But sometimes people don't have money for the clinics, especially out here, on the farms, so they call me. Not enough to live on, but…"

"Keeps you in the game." Seb gave his hand a squeeze. "So who's the patient?"

"Little Federica. Today you will see something I promise you have never seen before."

"I'm a city boy. That's not a tall order."

"*Si*. But even those who've lived in the country their whole lives have never seen a horse give birth to twins."

Andrea did his best Mario Andretti impersonation the rest of the way to Agriturismo Biologico Barone Flavio Vitale, a humble buttercup-yellow house nested in a grove of palm trees. A tween girl with a wispy topknot raced up to the SUV before Andrea could shift into park. Before long they were racing down a pebbled path, arms full of medical supplies, to an eerily quiet stable yard. A menagerie of animals—donkeys, rabbits, goats, chickens, even a couple fawns—hunkered down in their pens as if cowering from a gathering storm. An intense pair of border collies patrolled the area before the stable door, growling when Seb approached. A whistle from Andrea stood them down; they returned to their posts, ever vigilant.

A whinnying wail erupted from inside the small stable, triggering a chorus of upset from the animals. The girl held the door as they moved into the dark of the stable, its stalls empty except for the light of one half-shuttered lantern at the center of the aisle. A squat, round-faced woman with cheek-pinching hands welcomed Andrea. They whispered so softly as they hugged that Seb didn't catch her name despite introductions. A stricken teenaged boy nodded in Andrea's direction without taking his eyes off the mare in the main stall, who acknowledged them with another bellowing whinny. Andrea looked in on her, then reassured them in words that needed no translation: all was well.

The girl, Chiara, motioned them over to a small staging

area that already contained blankets, gloves, aprons, a handwashing station, sterile clamps, iodine, and… lube. Seb tried not to stare as Andrea set up his instruments and supplies, smiling awkwardly at his young hostess while Andrea chatted sotto voce with the owner, Renia. A steady stream of groans and huffs continued to echo out from the stall where the boy, the latest in a long line of Flavios, stood guard over his horse.

Just as he was starting to feel like a fifth wheel, Andrea pulled him aside and pushed an apron against his chest.

"Put this on," he whispered. "Looks more official. I told them you were doing your residence in Canada and just wanted to observe. Don't worry, I won't need your help. Federica is Flavio's horse. As you can see, he's very worried."

"Is she in danger?"

"Not right now, but… Twins in horses, it's very rare. One-in-ten-thousand chance. For both to be healthy, that is one in fifty thousand. More risk for the mare. Usually one of the foals spontaneously aborts and the pregnancy is lost. So this situation…"

"You've never done this before."

Andrea sighed. "No. And the vet who has been following Federica had an emergency, so I am the understudy in this little drama. But he took some scans a few weeks ago, and I have his notes… I think it will be okay."

Seb met his cautious smile with one of his own, clapped him on the back.

"I know it will."

"I am glad you are here."

"Me too."

"I hope it doesn't bother you that things might not go well…"

Seb clicked his tongue. "But they will, right? No negative talk."

"*Sì.* Very wise, Sebastiano." Andrea watched him for a few pregnant moments, checking for signs of doubt but also… admiring. Seb resisted the urge to snatch a kiss, felt his cheeks bloom. "Twins can be unpredictable, but otherwise she will only give birth under cover of night. So you might be in for a bit of a wait. If you ever want to go—"

"And miss catching lightning in a bottle? No way. Besides, the hay looks comfy."

"*Bene.* Just one thing to remember: we must stay very, very quiet. Federica must concentrate, and we don't want to bother her. It will seem like I'm not doing anything for a long time, but that is how it is. We wait, we watch until we are sure something is wrong."

"Got it. And so do you."

With a wink, Andrea directed him over to a spot at the far side of the stall door, away from the family but with a clear view of the action. Seb wasted no time looking in.

Federica, a magnificent chestnut mare, lay on a bed of glistening straw. Her protuberant belly was nearly the same length width-wise as she was from snout to hocks, as if she'd swallowed a wagon wheel. Seb wondered if she understood what exactly was about to occur. Andrea, who had changed into a surgical smock, sterilized and lubed up his arm. He felt along the side of her abdomen, then inserted his arm up the birth canal. When he nodded, young Flavio almost managed to smile.

The countdown had begun.

Four hours and a hearty pasta dinner later, they returned to the barn to find Federica's back legs and belly slick with amniotic fluid. Two little hooves poked out of the birth canal, covered in a translucent sac. Seb held his breath as the mare wriggled and groaned, waiting for he knew not what. After a grueling few minutes, a head popped out, followed swiftly by chest and rump. Chiara started to cheer, but her mother shushed her with a hiss.

All of Federica's energy seemed to drain out of her as she lay panting with her newborn foal. Andrea darted in to break the sac, clearing the foal's airway so he could draw in his first breaths. After thirty endless minutes, Seb scanned the faces of his companions, wondering why no one intervened to pull the second pair of little hooves out. Andrea glanced at the clock a few times, but not a wrinkle creased his brow. Young Flavio white-knuckled the top edge of the stall door, a racer waiting for the gunshot. Renia kept a weather eye on her son. Chiara had retreated to the hayloft for a better view. Swallowing his questions, Seb turned back to the primal scene.

Federica staggered to her feet. After a few shaky steps, the foal's hind legs slipped out, and the umbilical cord tore off.

Andrea held up a warning hand to hold them back as he snuck into the stall. After calming Federica, Andrea settled the newborn in a clean patch of hay. While Federica nuzzled her foal, he examined her, helping her expel the first placenta. Andrea reinserted his arm into the birth canal to check on the second twin. He schooled his face, but Seb knew Andrea well enough by now to note the tension in his mouth as he fought off a frown. Once he'd extricated his arm, he made a move toward Renia.

"No!" Flavio bleated, clamping his mouth shut before either adult could censure him. A piercing look from his mother popped the head of steam he'd been working on. Eyes wet, gnawing his bottom lip bloody, Flavio stayed put.

Andrea whispered his findings to Renia. He made a swishing gesture with two fingers that even Seb could read: the second foal was inverted. His experience showed in what happened next: he gave Flavio a series of instructions to keep his mind occupied, sent Renia off for some supplies, and asked Chiara to go supervise the other animals to spare her the sight of the worst-case scenario. Seb wasn't even sure if he was ready to bear witness to a stillbirth or other horrors. Both his money and his prayers were on Federica.

In the stall, Federica slumped back onto her side, wriggling and whinnying with shocking force. Seb didn't blame her; if he'd just given birth, he wouldn't be signing up for round two anytime soon, let alone less than an hour later.

Then she started kicking herself in the stomach.

Flavio wailed, but Andrea caught him before he could vault into the stall. He shooed Flavio out of the barn with some stern words, but had only gentle coos for Federica. Andrea guided her around and around the stall so that, Seb guessed, the second foal might realign itself. Federica whined throughout, her breaths whistling out her snout so sharply Seb was surprised they didn't emit steam.

By the time Renia returned, Federica was sluggish with exhaustion. Andrea waved her into the stall, instructing her to brace Federica against a wall while he attempted to realign the foal. Rapt, Seb held his breath as Andrea once again reached arm-deep into the birth canal.

Minutes flew by like seconds. Seb leaned over the door's top edge, willing Andrea to succeed, the little foal to fight harder, the mare to endure. He was engrossed by the heavyweight bout between life and death, by Andrea wrestling with such primitive forces. A pointed look between Andrea and Renia had him biting his cheek to keep from crying out and getting exiled to the barnyard.

Seb's heart pounded as Andrea pulled out his surgical knife. He stared in disbelief as Andrea slashed open the sac inside Federica, tied a length of rope around the foal's hind legs, and, with a signal to Renia, yanked it out. The newborn foal landed in the hay beside her hour-old twin, unmoving. Andrea hurried to clear her airway. No response. With a feather-light touch in wild contrast with the violence of her birth, Andrea tickled her snout. This bit of veterinarian magic sparked her breathing, and she let out a soft snuffle.

Seb was shocked afterward to discover eight hours had passed since their arrival. By this time, both foals—a boy and a girl, names TBD—had taken their first steps and their first suckle, and Federica, unsurprisingly, slept. After sending a reluctant Flavio off to bed, Andrea gave both foals a quick but meticulous examination. Despite the language barrier, even Seb could tell he detailed care instructions to Renia.

Seb stayed silent throughout. The reverence of the moment suffused his head and his heart with a sense of calm. The barn had become a temple, and him a witness to a tradition as old as time itself yet as foreign as an ancient civilization. That afternoon he'd been sipping his espresso and planning a typical vacation day. Hours later he'd watched while two bright spirits entered the world. Three years ago he'd been doing something mundane—the shock of what came after had kicked the memory right out of his skull—when the police knocked on his door, changing him forever. Life didn't wait on your permission, your readiness. It threw you in the deep end to either sink or swim.

"You can come in," Andrea said once Renia had rushed off to fulfill some request of his. "Put on your apron and sterilize your hands. They are very fragile."

Seb hesitated a moment, not sure whether he should intrude on the little family, but eventually he did as suggested. He wouldn't get a second chance.

"Are they all right?"

"A bit small, but that's normal. Horses are really not made for carrying two foals." He gestured for Seb to greet Federica before attempting to pet the newborns. "To be honest, I didn't expect them both to survive. You brought us good luck."

Embarrassed, Seb quipped, "Ancient Japanese horse-saving technique."

"I thought you were Canadian."

"When convenient. Are they in any danger?"

"The next two weeks will be important. It's really up to Federica. She needs to make enough milk to feed both of them. There are things we can do if she doesn't, but it's risky. They are already small. If one of them doesn't get enough to eat…" He patted the colt's rump. "But Renia has dealt with all kinds of problems before. She will do what's best for them. If she weren't so experienced, her regular vet would have recommended termination. But instead, *per grazia di Dio*, here we are."

"And what an amazing place it is." Seb reached out a tentative hand, stroked across the filly's flank. Downy soft, if a bit sticky, he fell hard for the little miracle. "Thank you for bringing me here. I can't put into words how much it means to me."

Beaming, Andrea leaned in, and brushed a promise of a kiss over his lips.

Chapter Seven

Heavy orchard boughs
Ripe with fragrant, fatted fruit
Shade to lovers' bliss
-#73, *In Blue Solitudes*, S. Wilson-Osaki

Seb had reached the fourth stage of discovery, exhilaration, by the time they broke off the path to stroll between rows of fruit trees. Late-summer peaches and blood oranges sagged their leafy branches for maximum shade, though a few overripe divers got squashed underfoot. Seb moved closer to Andrea to twine their fingers, unable to resist swinging their joined hands. Giddy with leisure, Seb snatched a fat peach from a passing bough and ripped into its juicy flesh.

"How can you eat?" Andrea asked when offered a bite. Once the little horse family had settled in for the night, Renia laid out a banquet fit for her royal ancestors. They bunked in one of the guest rooms, too glutted on food and excitement to do more than kiss good night, let alone strip, before collapsing into slumber. Fortified by a lavish breakfast and a bracing swim, Renia had invited them to explore the property before the long drive back.

"How can you not?" Seb gulped in another mouthful, juices running down his chin. "Although if you recall, I didn't have a second slice of *crostata*."

"You had two helpings of museli and four *zeppole*. Does some kind of Italian food ghost visit you at night, leading you from feast to feast but not letting you eat?"

"Three of them. Armed with bags of seashells and an endless supply of G&Ts."

Andrea laughed, tugging him close and hooking his arm around Seb's waist. He was a good half foot taller than his stealth veterinarian, so Seb slung his arm around Andrea's shoulders, relaxed against him. Andrea's wavy hair tickled the delicate patch on the underside of his elbow. Their hips locked into place like the final pieces of a puzzle. Seb wanted to howl, to sing, to cry out to all the ancient gods for giving him this day.

Instead he tore off another strip of peach, crushed out its tart ambrosia. Sparkles of sunlight between the leaves heightened the otherworldly atmosphere, as if they'd slipped through to another dimension. The scent of sweet citrus accented Andrea's earthy musk, tinged with antiseptic soap. They stumbled over a tree root, fell into each another. With that sinuous body pressed against his, a new kind of appetite stirred.

Dropping the peach, Seb tipped Andrea's bold Roman jaw upward, gazed into the face that inspired so much confusion and longing in him. Nectar-spiked blood coursed through his veins, rousing his too-long-dormant desire. Seb thumbed the length of Andrea's bottom lip, his own parted, panting. Andrea stilled, not inviting but not rejecting. Giving

Seb all the space in the world, though they were only inches apart.

Did he dare disturb the universe?

He did.

Andrea's lips, soft and plump as Seb's discarded peach, welcomed him. Stubble fuzz scratched the edges of Seb's mouth as he gave over to the kiss, learning new steps in a familiar dance. A sharp sigh of relief escaped Andrea when he opened to him, hugged his arms up Seb's back, dug his fingers into his shoulders. A lash of Andrea's tongue lured Seb in deeper, heated breaths and heady musk mingling in his singular taste.

This was not Henry's tyrannical command of Seb's body and mind, which Seb had been more than eager to obey. Where Henry had demanded, Andrea urged. Where he claimed, Andrea conceded. Both lit Seb's wick, but only Andrea's total submission had him thick as a stick of dynamite, embarrassingly ready to blow.

Three years of suppressed need surged in him now. Seb cupped Andrea's head and drank greedily, twisting his fingers in the black ivy strands of his hair. A moan reverberated down his spine, squeezed the first slickness from his cock. Andrea pulled them chest to chest, ground his denim-clad erection into Seb's hip.

The mellow sun suddenly scorched, searing his scalp and roasting Seb in his sweat-slick sarong. He dragged Andrea into the shade of a lemon tree, peeling off his shirt before shoving him against the trunk. Andrea sought his mouth as if needing him to breathe, guiding Seb's hands to his belt and gripping his wrists as he tore at the buckle. Red silk boxers bulged against the buttons of his fly. Seb stole a moment to admire the view—Andrea's sculpted pecs and tantalizing treasure trail leading him like a bull to the matador's flag-covered sword.

Seb groped Andrea's cock, bit into his neck. He cursed in at least two languages, bucking into Seb's hand. Seb spied a dark-rose nipple in a briar of darker hair, but Andrea was primed and panting. A stain bloomed at the head of his tented boxers. Seb's heavy tongue wanted nothing but salt. He dropped to his knees, freed Andrea's erection from its satin sheath. Pressed his face into his groin until his every sense was saturated in Andrea's essence.

Seb glanced up at his sweet veterinarian maddened with lust. Eyes blown wide at the sight of Seb at his service, they begged him for mercy but would not dare a nudge of encouragement. So different from anyone he had been with before, but somehow just what Seb needed. He wondered just how long it had been for Andrea, considered teasing him into a right frenzy. Instead he smiled, then licked up the length of his cock.

And moaned. How had he gone without this for so long? The feel of a lover tensing and trembling at every swipe of his tongue. The texture of his shaft as Seb licked up that prominent vein. The thrill of taking Andrea's cock all the way down his throat. Seb sucked in his cheeks as he pulled off to knead Andrea's plum-fat balls, wanting more. Wanting everything: to spin him around and lave his puckered hole; to work one finger, then two, then three into him; to spread him wide and fuck him senseless; to bore so deep into his sun-kissed body that he bathed in the font of his spirit.

Andrea clutched at the nape of Seb's neck, cried out. Seb swallowed every last drop of his seed, giddy with laughter as he gave him a last lingering lick, then staggered to his feet. Seb purred as Andrea tended to him, his orgasm almost an afterthought, the climactic firework on the Fourth of July. He still hummed as Andrea wrapped him in a full-body embrace, gentled his lips with a much more languid kiss.

"You okay?"

Seb hated the hesitation in his voice. "Tremendous. You?"

A soft chuckle ticked his collar. "As if you need to ask."

Seb shook his head, unable to help feeling smug. And hungry for more. Now that his sensual appetite had returned, it seemed he wouldn't be sated by anything short of devouring Andrea whole.

"Come back to my place?"

He felt more than saw the stretch of Andrea's smile. "Just want to check on Federica one more time."

"Sure. I can wait."

"That makes one of us."

The promise of his lips had Seb counting the seconds.

Seb felt Andrea's eyes on him as he slipped off the bed and meandered over to the window, throwing the latch to open the shutters wide. Only a whisper of a breeze snuck into the bedroom, enough to cool Seb's overheated skin. He leaned over the sill, inhaled deep of the evening air. Tourists from the hotels up the hillside road staggered down to dinner, their flip-flops and running shoes replaced with high heels and sandals, which didn't fare so well on an incline.

Across the way, the same middle-aged Italian woman as always sat framed by her balcony door, still as a portrait, forever watching the world go by. Seb recognized in her a kindred spirit. Until a few days ago, he'd been stuck in a similar pantomime of life, going through the motions under a veil of perpetual grief. Now, navel sticky with their recent eruptions and muscles still drunk on afterglow, he shuffled off to the bathroom to fetch a washcloth, barely recognizing the grinning, bright-eyed fool in the mirror.

Andrea stole the damp cloth from him as soon as he crawled back up the bed, tending quickly to himself before taking his time cleaning Seb. Even after he'd settled in against Seb's side, head hovering over his shoulder until Seb eased him down with a pet, Andrea continued to map the planes and hollows of his chest, his arms, his hips, his thighs, a sensual cartographer dedicated to his craft. Seb gave over to these ministrations, but didn't have it in him to reciprocate. After two blazing, breathless bouts, it would be a while before his flame could be lit.

Instead Seb nested his nose in Andrea's hair, stroked his thumb across late-afternoon neck stubble. Luxuriated in the moment.

They barely spoke on the way back from the *agriturismo* ranch, neither willing to crack the thickening skein of desire that covered them in the wake of their first encounter.

Andrea rested his hand on Seb's knee when not busy with the clutch, shifting his excitement into higher and higher gears as deftly as he maneuvered the SUV. They came together at those endless stoplights, necking like teens on their first visit to makeout point. Only the blare of a horn would break them apart—laughing, shame-faced but unrepentant. By the time they pulled up to the Villa Napolitana, Seb was practically in Andrea's lap.

He never thought he'd scale those stairs so quick. They broke into the apartment in a tangle of limbs, stripping as they climbed to the loft. The hour-long drive back had made them desperate; they vaulted onto the bed midkiss, Seb's ankles still shackled by his briefs. Andrea was just as deliciously pliant as in their first round, matching Seb grind for grind, thrust for thrust, but letting him set the rhythm. A bit of backdoor mischief had him speaking in tongues. Seb planned to explore Andrea's operatic side further on the next go-around. The chance to play conductor had awakened something primal in him. Watching Andrea sing out his last prompted his climax, ecstasy and pride ringing through Seb as he collapsed.

"Wine, *bello*?"

Andrea made a poor show of hiding his smile at the term of endearment. "Mmm." He took his time easing away from Seb, plucking a kiss from behind his ear before retreating to the kitchen.

Fifteen minutes later Seb wondered if he'd somehow gotten lost in a two-room apartment. He resisted the temptation to yank on a pair of boxers as he went to look for him, wished he had when he found Andrea frozen in front of the picture of Henry Seb had stupidly tacked to the fridge door.

Seb took a deep, centering breath, went to the counter, poured the wine. Only exhaled when Andrea accepted his glass, hooked an arm around his waist.

"How are you feeling?"

"Good." Seb didn't have to force his smile. "Great. Best day in… Well, in three years. Although if you'd told me then the key to getting over Henry would be watching a horse give birth…" A twinge of worry tugged between his shoulder blades when Andrea didn't laugh.

"Why do you keep him down here? I would have thought…"

"He wouldn't mind, if that's what you're getting at." Seb tucked him under his arm, steered them toward the stairs. "He would have wanted me to move on. Probably a lot sooner. This is going to sound funny, but… I just didn't want him to see it. It's one thing to wish it—"

"And another to witness."

"Exactly." That twinge became a pinch when Andrea halted them before the bottom step. "Do you mind?"

"What? No, no. I…" He drew away to look Seb in the eye. "I knew him."

Seb felt all the air rush out of his lungs. "What do you mean? You… *knew him*, knew him?"

"No, no, not like that. I drove him. From the airport and other places. But his name was not Henry…"

"Walter Bishop," Seb confirmed. "He used a fake name when researching a travel guide so that hotel and restaurant owners didn't recognize him."

"Ah!" After a full-body sigh, Andrea sagged against him. "Of course."

Seb chuckled, welcomed him back in. "This was when, ten years ago? You couldn't have been more than—"

"Nineteen. And very confused. But seeing someone like Wally, who was…" He waved his free hand, sloshed wine on the floor.

"Gay as a French trombone?"

Andrea snorted. "He didn't hide."

"Couldn't. But that's what drew me in. He was a beacon."

Andrea glanced back at the picture. "He made me realize things were possible. That I could be as I am and still survive in the world. We talked one night at my aunt's trattoria. It's because of him that I came out to my family. I'll never forget that night."

Seb nodded, started back up the stairs. "He loved people. That's what made him so good at his job. As a writer he was… well, a bit of a mess. But he could make the contacts, strike up a conversation, do the kinds of things people want to when they go on vacation. And he had the good sense to marry an editor."

"He must have been gone a lot."

"Made up for it when he was home." Seb sat against the backboard so Andrea could scoot in between his legs and recline against his chest. He found these confessions easier if they weren't face-to-face. "It was different back then, when we were dating. Once we got married, he took shorter assignments. The irony is he was a few weeks away from starting a new job when he…" Seb shut his eyes, sat with his sadness until the words came. "We wanted kids. He needed to be around more for that to happen. He was almost done. Just one short trip to this new hotel in Banff. He was leaving the next day. But then..."

Andrea turned around, hugged him.

"But that's in the past." Seb found solace in that solemn gaze. But he wanted something more. "Here's to the present."

They clinked glasses, but Andrea still looked too pensive for Seb's liking.

"And the future?"

"Will take care of itself. The plan right now is no plans, no expectations, except for... Oh! Tomorrow's Saturday, right? We already have a date."

"Ah, yes! *Calcio!*" Finally Seb caught a glint off Andrea's pearly whites. "What do you play? Forward? Defense? Goal?"

"Head cheerleader." He demurred when Andrea groaned. "I don't have any pom-poms, but I will bring my squad. You may come to regret inviting us. We are loud."

"And proud?"

Remembering the fight in the parking lot the other day, Seb thought better of his quip. "Very. But I don't want to make things harder for you."

Andrea chuckled. "That is very kind of you. But this is, uh... a rainbow team. We've all been kicked out of our local clubs."

"For being queer?"

"Not officially, but you know how it is."

"Now I wish I did have pom-poms."

Andrea planted a kiss in the center of his chest. "Just wear that… What is it, a kilt?"

"My sarong?"

"Yes. Wear that."

Even beneath such a deep tan, Seb traced the blush that spread across his cheeks. "Like it, do you?"

Andrea cleared his throat, dodged his inquisitive look. "It suits you."

"Ah. Good to know. Any part of me in particular?"

"*Sì.* Your ass."

At Seb's howl of laughter, Andrea threw a decorative pillow at his head.

Chapter Eight

STALLIONS JOSTLING DOWN
THE VERDANT PITCH, UPROOTING
BLADES OF GRASS, RIVALS
-#131, *In Blue Solitudes*, S. Wilson-Osaki

Little more than a strip of green sandwiched between former cloisters on the beach road, the *calcio* "playing field" had no goal posts, no benches, and no lines. Nothing to distinguish it from, say, Seb's front lawn, other than its postcard-pretty surroundings and the motley group at its center.

As he and the ladies paraded down the center of the road, high-chinned and haughty as visiting royalty, flocks of tourists parted to laugh, to wave, to cheer, or just to gawk. True daughters of New Orleans, the ladies had bedecked themselves in their most colorful dresses and hats, with shell and dried chili necklaces in place of beads and feathers. In her tasseled flapper-style dress and severe head-banned bob, Ceri channeled Louise Brooks via the French Quarter. With exaggerated makeup and sequined everything, Kath was a parade float come to life. Maya, meanwhile, played mysterious in jewel tones with a harlequin mask on the end of a lorgnette (formerly a selfie stick). Seb's wardrobe didn't quite match their level of flash, but he'd donned what he nicknamed his centurion sarong with a see-through tank and wrapped a few chilies around his man bun. Though he faked it till he made it, part of him wondered if the players would ban them from the field for being too out there.

He needn't have worried.

Saturday-morning soccer proved to be quite the enterprise for the makeshift team. Some ran laps while others spread chalk. A few stretched. The referee distributed kerchiefs to designate sides, and two lumbersexuals took care of the goal posts. Deck chairs had already been divided into color-coded groups that made for a bisected Italian flag, white/red or green/black.

"I hope they have a 'fabulous' section," Kath declared as they veered off onto the grass, a few curious tourists straggling in their wake.

"Or a fainting couch." Maya's mask dropped as she ogled the man candy. "I do declare. Why hasn't Andrea introduced us to any of these friends before now?"

"Because they don't play for your team," Ceri reminded her in her best Dorothy Parker drawl. "Mine, however..."

A healthy sprinkling of women peppered both sides, one of which, Seb noticed, was Lucia. *Generalissimo* Matto, eager to play mascot, zipped around the field, barking orders at the setup crew.

Seb nudged Ceri with his elbow. "You should go thank her. For yesterday."

She stared him down over the top edge of her sunglasses. "I didn't realize auditions for the part of Yente in *Fiddler on the Roof* were still open."

"I'm paying it forward." Seb winked in Maya's direction. "Learned from the best."

"Oh, come now," Kath clucked. "With instincts like yours, you must be self-taught." She caught her sister mid-eye-roll to urge, "You heard the man. Go talk to her!"

Ceri huffed. "No need to light a fire. Unlike this one, my groove hasn't gone anywhere. Watch and learn."

The beaded fringe of her dress tinkled as she shimmied over to Lucia.

"Where's your beau, cher?" Maya inquired.

"Incoming." Seb was relieved Andrea's smile reached all the way up to his eyes. "And don't call him that."

"Sweetie," Kath whispered, "you need to scratch off the 'Now' and make him Mr. Right. Just look at those—"

"*Signore!*" Andrea welcomed them with smooches and hugs that almost turned Seb the color of the turf. But then he used his cheering squad as a shield for some alone time with Seb's best sarong-clad asset, and all was forgiven. "And you, Sebastiano? I see you got your beauty rest."

Andrea, short a driver since he'd sidelined his Cousin Bruno, had snuck out around 5:00 a.m. for three airport runs before the game. Seb wasn't sure if he was more impressed by his dedication or how delectable he looked after three hours' sleep.

"I hope your play is as smooth as your tongue, Sorrentino."

"You'll have to let me know after the match."

"That's a promise."

A chorus of "oohs" from his squad heralded the rest of

the players, who begged introductions from Andrea and admired their flamboyant fashion. Magnanimous as ever, Andrea introduced Seb to 80 percent of the gay men in Amalfi without a flicker of hesitation. Seb wasn't sure whether to be concerned or impressed by this show of confidence. He was too preoccupied with watching for signs of which, if any, were former lovers. Not that he had any right to be jealous.

Not that that had ever stopped him before.

After a playful argument over whose side they would cheer for, Seb and the ladies settled into their red-and-white seats, parasols deployed against the noontime sun. Ceri, having completed her first round of flirtation, passed around a flask of gin because in Amalfi, it was never too early.

The players took their sides, huddling up to discuss strategy. Only then did Seb realize he didn't even know what Andrea played. He made a game of guessing as the ladies picked their favorites, trying to relate each position to bedroom preference. Seb ended up biting a knuckle to stifle his laughter, which did not go unnoticed by his hawkeyed companions.

"Are you going to join in the festivities, cher? Or is your private party invite-only?" Maya asked, side-eye in full effect.

Seb gave them the Andrea-less version of his theory. The resulting cackles got them scolded by the ref.

"So center forward, most dominant? Something like that?" Kath queried.

"I was thinking more willing to go the distance for as long as it takes to get you there," Seb replied.

"But not inventive," Maya added.

"No. That's a halfback. Has to be everything to everyone, so has all the skills."

"Sounds like my ex-husband," Kath chuckled. "And I mean *everyone*."

Ceri gave her shoulder a squeeze.

"Striker hammers it out, no muss, no fuss, no foreplay." Seb smirked at their collective groan.

"Been there," Ceri said.

"Wore the T-shirt," Maya agreed.

"Defense…" Kath rubbed her hands together. "Hmm. I'm guessing good, giving, and game."

Seb nodded. "It's not a glamour position. But sweeper's the one you really want on your side. Or, er, between your sheets."

"Can I just say this is the most fun I've ever had watching competitive sports?" Ceri commented.

Ignoring her sister, Kath asked Seb, "And why is that, sugar?"

"Because they go the extra mile. They're the last line of defense, the ones who get you out of the tightest spots. You have to make sure to think of their needs because all they think of is you."

"Oh, my!" Maya fanned herself. "I like a bit more steel in my partners, but every so often, a lady has to treat herself."

"Sweepers live to serve," Seb confirmed.

They fell silent a moment, each daydreaming intimate scenarios with their preferred player position. The trill of the whistle shocked them out of their reverie.

"Game's about to start," Kath urged. "Goalie."

"Puts up a wall and won't let anything through. Aloof. Arrogant. Technically proficient—so the sex might be hot, but he's out of bed the second you're done."

"Genius, cher." Maya bussed him on the cheek.

"I think you mean 'Gerardo,'" Kath teased.

"I smell a self-help book," Ceri complimented. "Maybe you've got some love guru in you after all."

"He's like a genie," Maya added. "Give him a good, long rub—"

"Hold the phone, ladies." Kath eyed them each in turn, tongue tucked in the corner of her lip like the cat that got the cream. "Predictions. Which one is *Bello* Andrea?"

They all turned to Seb, who smiled with Buddha-like serenity. "All will be revealed." He waved his hands toward the field with a magician's flourish.

They played eight a side: one center, two wings, one halfback, two defense, a sweep, and a goalie. A heated debate preoccupied the defensive line of Andrea's team until the first bleep of the whistle, then, as Seb secretly predicted, Andrea backed up toward the goal to placate the other two. A sweep, then.

Seb straightened in his seat, fighting an ear-to-ear grin. The ladies waved and cheered for Andrea, each stealing a moment to wink at Seb. He cupped his hands around his mouth and shouted, "*Vai, vai! Bianco e rosso!*" Then a coin was flipped, the ball passed, and the game was on.

The advantage ping-ponged back and forth the first part of the half as the teams found their rhythm. The players knew each others' strengths and weaknesses too well, and most still worked off a hangover. Andrea's steady gaze locked on to the ball, but it didn't come close to penetrating past either team's line of defense.

Not invested in the outcome beyond Andrea having a good game, Seb had no complaints. Especially given the view. In team colors, Andrea somehow soared to a whole new level of handsomeness. If Seb ever saw him in a tux, he might pass out.

But a James Bond he wasn't. Or a Henry Wilson, for that matter. The real Andrea Sorrentino had a hundred acquaintances but few real friends, compromised his dream to support his mother and sister, stuck his hand into a laboring horse to save her colt. Advertised for local businesses but confided hard truths to the discerning tourist. Chided his cousin for lack of work ethic but played hooky on occasion. Had a reputation for being a hard-ass at the taxi rank but conceded to his teammates on the soccer field. A generous, compassionate, vibrant man Seb had gotten to know far better than a vacation fling.

"I take it, Agent Osaki, that Operation Stella is nearing completion?" Maya whispered to him when Kath and Ceri moved to the sideline to perform a cheer from their high school days. Because of course Kath had been on a squad.

"The first mission was a definite win for our side," Seb cagily replied, "but the outcome remains unpredictable."

"Regrets?"

"No, no. Just…" He struggled to explain, hiding behind the metaphor. "I got more intel than I know what to do with, I guess."

"You're going in again?"

Seb smiled to himself. "Oh, yeah. As soon as possible."

Maya inhaled deeply, considering.

"Don't lose sight of your objective: fun. Getting back to yourself but also becoming the new you. Find a happy medium between your inner Michael and Brian. As for the outcome… that's kind of inevitable, isn't it? So watch yourself." Her gaze drifted over to the field. "It's not like you don't have options."

Seb ignored the flare of panic the thought of multiple vacation flings sent up. He really was a Michael at heart. "I prefer to go out on a win."

"One-man guy? I get you."

"Again with the Rufus Wainwright."

"Ain't broke, don't fix it." She patted him on the knee, then squeezed. "Take care with that one. He's a sweep, after all."

Seb couldn't help a bawdy laugh. "You have no idea."

At the halftime whistle, the teams huddled around their respective water coolers to discuss strategy. Kath surreptitiously passed around the flask, not wanting to distract the players with the promise of libations. Given the looks of intense concentration on their faces when they were supposed to be relaxing, Seb was pretty sure most would have refused on principle. The Gods of *Calcio* might smite anyone indulging in a little hair of the dog.

The snarl of a motorbike engine broke through the hum of the coastal road traffic. A spike of panic shot up Seb's spine. He glanced up in time to see three bikes ripping down the hillside Via Matteo Camera. Helmetless and hell-bent, they skidded around cars and up side walls before disappearing into a small tunnel. Seb was on his feet before he knew it, tracking them while trying to rein in his galloping heart. Horn blasts, tire squeals, and cursing heralded their demolition derby through the Piazza Flavio Gioia.

Against traffic they bombed down the Via Lungomare dei Cavalieri, seconds from the soccer field. One jackknifed onto the beachside boardwalk to honk its way through groups of tourists. Another streaked by at breakneck speed, popping a wheelie.

"Move!" Everything in Seb screamed at him to flee; instead Maya dragged him onto the field seconds before one of the bikes crashed through the back row of chairs.

"*Ricchioni!*" Andrea's cousin Bruno shouted before spitting on the grass.

The other two bikers zoomed over, armed with bushels of tomatoes they stole from a vendor. Jeering and calling them homophobic slurs that needed no translation, they pelted the red-and-white players with the ripe, squishy fruit. Seb stood paralyzed, every tomato blast like a stone on his chest. His throat cinched and his feet leaden, he fought for every gasp, powerless as Cousin Bruno and his gang of hooligans bullied his friends.

Brave little Matto, the only one able to dodge the tomatoes, charged at them, diving for their tires. When one of them tried to kick him back, Matto chomped down on his ankle. The driver's howl distracted the others long enough for Andrea and his gang to spring into action, grabbing the water cooler and drenching Bruno with it. A parasol-wielding Kath stalked up to the third biker and swatted him until he sped off.

At Lucia's whistle, calling Matto to heel, the scarred

biker took a powder, leaving only drenched, furious Bruno versus a livid crowd. Both teams assembled to berate him, with Andrea the soprano of the discordant choir. Seb's throat unclenched when he spied Andrea winding up his arm for a slap. Sucking in a few lungfuls of air, Seb shoved through the crowd, grabbing Andrea by the wrist just in time.

Andrea shot him a death look, then, when he saw who it was, deflated. Muttering a curse under his breath, he gave Bruno a final warning in Italian, then instructed his teammates to let him go. With a few choice hand gestures and a defiant rev of his engine, Bruno peeled off to terrorize more tourists.

"You all right?" Andrea asked *him,* half of his face splattered with tomato gore. "You've gone gray."

"Says the Phantom of the Soccer Field." Seb reached up to slick back a dripping forelock. "Did he get you in the head? Let me grab a towel."

The ladies were already on the case, distributing face wipes and Tide to Go to the "wounded." By the time Seb nabbed some, Andrea had been drawn aside by some of the other players. The clench to his jaw and the tension in his brow told Seb he was once again bearing the burden of his cousin's crimes. Seb bristled in sympathy, wishing he'd spent more time with those Italian language tapes.

The familiar scent of a Gauloise heralded Ceri, who fell in beside him. She offered him a haul; touched, he took it. Only then did he notice Matto in her arms, blood—or more likely tomato—on his mouth. He craned his head over her shoulder to growl at the traffic, eager for round two.

"They're not calling the police," Ceri sighed, and Seb understood why she'd sought him out. The thought seared hotter than the smoke across his tongue. He expelled both in a long, controlled stream.

"I'm guessing it's not the first time."

"Give the man a prize."

Seb nodded, fighting to dispel the echo of screeching tires from his mind.

"Sometimes the only thing to do is… move past it."

Ceri snatched back her cigarette with a sharp tug, took a long drag. "Too damn often."

As if on cue, the referee's whistle trilled, and the players jogged back into position.

Two hours later all lingering fears or worries had been silenced, Italian-style, by good company and other earthly pleasures.

Seb popped another fried calamari into his mouth, savoring the salty, briny crunch. Washed it down with a sip of espresso. Not as satisfying as a swig of beer, but if he wanted to keep up with his slick-haired Italian jock—and getting Andrea alone dominated his thoughts as much as the white-and-red team had the match—he had to counteract all that gin. With that in mind, Seb scooped up a few oysters and headed out to the small piazza for some air.

The *calcio* club's weekly afterparty had taken over a grotty hole-in-the-wall backstreet café no over-baked tourist would dare invade. Like the best local watering holes, the dim lights, threadbare tables and booths, and overabundance of neon signs promised little except for low-low prices and shady corners in which to make mischief. Seb wished he could lure Andrea into one, but his sexy sweep busied himself with—what else?—making sure everyone was happy.

One could be forgiven for assuming Andrea was part of the wait staff. He ferried trays of food from the kitchen while the actual waiter chatted up Kath and fetched drinks from the overwhelmed bartender. Like the perfect host, every spare moment found him checking on one of the groups, during which someone would inevitably lead him to the side for a private airing of grievances. He'd spent a good twenty minutes in the washroom looking over the hero of the day, Matto, despite Lucia's protests. Andrea even kept an appointment schedule in his pocket so he could pencil in someone's ailing pet.

Work hustle Seb understood. Those odd jobs paid the bills. But Andrea hadn't sat down since they arrived almost two hours ago, and Seb considered staging an intervention.

He couldn't, of course, and not just because of how it would look, even in an LGBTQ-friendly crowd. He had no claim on Andrea and never would. To demand more intimacy from him while plotting to steal him away for the night was beyond spoiled brat. Anything Seb did or said would live on for Andrea post-tryst. Seb felt the responsibility of that as heavily as he imagined Andrea did his duty to his friends and family.

Which was not to say Seb minded when someone nicked

the last oyster from his plate.

"Your ladies know how to enjoy themselves," Andrea remarked, leaning on the same pillar as Seb.

Seb watched him slurp down his oyster, the bob of his Adam's apple doing things to his concentration. He tore away his stare to pick out the ladies in the crowd. Done with the waiter, Kath sat in a circle of younger players, holding court with den-mother fondness. Maya whooped it up at the bar with four studs. Seb hoped for her sake at least one of them was bi. At the far end, Ceri downed shots and made goo-goo eyes at Lucia, whom he fully expected to find at breakfast the next morning. Matto snoozed under Lucia's stool, looking like he'd already had one too many.

He shrugged. "Amalfi."

Andrea laughed, hip-checked him. "You're learning."

"From the best."

"And you? Not so good with crowds?"

"I was looking for my date."

"He left you alone? With all these hot guys around? *Bastardo*."

Seb snorted. "I know! Temptation everywhere I turn. He's lucky I'm not like that."

"Oh? Like what?"

"Wouldn't you like to know."

"I think maybe I would. Perhaps we can go somewhere… quieter." Andrea pushed off the pillar, turned so they were face-to-face. Leaned in suggestively, making the most of Seb's slumped posture. Dark glints of desire flecked his eyes as he locked them on Seb. "You could show me."

A slow smile spread across Seb's lips, but he held his

tongue. Waited for the air to sizzle, for Andrea to blink, for the kiss to come. Reading Seb like the skilled player he was, Andrea resisted, hovering just close enough for their skin to tingle, their breaths to quicken, their bodies to arch toward each other, linked together by the invisible current that had powered up the moment they'd met. Eagerness and arousal zapped every nerve to attention, the pull of their attraction magnetizing Seb. They fought against it, thrilling at the buzz of tension in every muscle, every limb—all building toward a sensual lightning strike.

Andrea winced, shuddered. Inched closer, his resolve shaking. Seb deepened his smile, moved to meet him—

The trill of a cell phone broke the spell. Andrea sighed, dug into his pocket. The green light of the screen turned his Italian coloring a jaundiced shade as he took in the name. He cursed, then answered, giving Seb an apologetic squeeze on the arm before pacing farther into the piazza.

"*Sì, Zia.*"

Seb understood the exchange that followed through Andrea's expressions, first sympathy, then anger, then exasperation, then finally acceptance, all peppered with several guilty glances in Seb's direction. In short his evening had just been ruined. The string of muttered curses he spat out after hanging up did nothing to correct Seb's reading of the conversation. Neither did Andrea's face when he turned back to him.

Seb held his hands up in a pacifying gesture. "It's okay."

"No, it's not."

"He's your cousin. He's family. I get it."

"How did you know?"

"Have I neglected to mention my latent psychic ability?"

Andrea didn't even smirk. "Does that mean you can strangle someone without putting your hands on them?"

"That's telekinesis, so no." He approached Andrea cautiously, wary of poking an angry bear. Instead this one turned cuddly the moment he offered him his arms. "Can I see you after?"

He saw Andrea consider and reject a dozen scenarios in less than a minute. "That depends."

"On what?"

"How you feel about meeting my family."

To his surprise, no pinch of nervous panic stabbed Seb between the eyes. "How would *you* feel about that?"

He felt Andrea start, straighten in his arms. "After this afternoon, you would be okay with it?"

"I don't scare that easy. And Bruno's not your entire family. Anyway, your mom sounds amazing. Especially her food. Will there be food?"

At that, Andrea did laugh. "Enough to fill a second stomach."

"Sounds great to me. But… tell me the truth, Dre. Are *you* ready for this?"

"I…" A war of expressions battled across his face, too many for Seb to track. But the victorious one made Seb's heart swell a little too big for his chest. "I don't want to miss a night with you. Maybe it's stupid of me to admit that, but… it's true."

If there was any stupid between them, it was the grin on Seb's face. It was delving deeper into the whirlpool of this man's life with no tether to reel Seb back in.

"Then what's the plan?"

"We need to get going. We're catching the ferry to Capri."

Chapter Nine

BIRTHED FROM THE DEEP,
VULCAN'S THUNDER-FORGED PEARL
FLOATS SERENELY
-#8, *In Blue Solitudes*, S. WILSON-OSAKI

Two hours later Seb craned so far over the rail of the ferry's upper deck that he almost swan-dived onto the boardwalk. A lava flow of tourists poured out of every door and archway in Capri's Marina Grande, bubbling around the bus stops, docked boats, and funicular entrance as a wave of newcomers drained out. Beyond the row of multicolored shops and restaurants across the way, a lush green landscape wrapped around one middling and one soaring peak. If the Amalfi Coast was a paradise fit for a queen, this was its crown jewel.

The clunk of the ferry against the dock signaled their arrival. Andrea, nonplussed by a place he'd been to a thousand times, chatted with one of the stewards. He gestured in Seb's direction in answer to a question, shrugged in that Italian way. The steward put his hands up like paws and stuck out his tongue.

"What?" Seb called over.

"He says you are like a dog out a car window."

With last look at the view, Seb pushed off the rail and joined Andrea.

"Nothing wrong with a little enthusiasm." He added as much innuendo into his tone as he could, but Andrea only rolled his eyes. "Haven't heard you complain."

"Don't be cheesy."

The steward did his best impression of a deer in the headlights.

"Aren't you going to translate that?" Seb asked, smirking.

"Let's get going."

They followed the steward and snuck off the boat first, not that the advantage helped in navigating the dense crowd. Andrea clamped a hand on his shoulder to better steer him toward the transportation hub, squeezing tighter and tighter as the stress of the afternoon returned. Seb had managed to distract him during the ferry ride with his puppylike antics, but now that they closed in on his aunt's restaurant, his jaw was so tight Seb feared he might crack a tooth. To say nothing of how he dug his palm into the muscle of Seb's shoulder blade. If Andrea got any tenser, Seb would have to find a toilet stall where he could perform some mouth-to-cock resuscitation.

"Are we going dick or balls?" he asked as they huddled into the line for the funicular, which spilled into the street, blocking traffic.

"Huh?"

Seb pointed at the big hill, then at the two smaller hills. Andrea huffed a laugh, shook his head.

"Come on, smile, *bello*." Seb surreptitiously pinched his ass. "You can do it."

"We're going to be late."

"You're doing them the favor. I think they'll forgive you this time."

"You haven't met them yet."

Seb scrutinized him. "Was this a bad idea? Do you want me to play tourist till you're done?"

The immediate panic that splashed across Andrea's face relieved Seb.

"No, no. I..." Andrea let out a heavy sigh. "I want you to meet them. I just see all these people, and I know they must already be drowning."

Seb glanced around for a quicker way up the hill, but the clogged roads and endless lines for the bus made the funicular line—which, once you were in the thick of it, moved regularly—their best option.

"Which is probably what your cousin thought when he hightailed it for the mainland this morning."

Andrea scoffed. "*Sì*."

As they neared the door, the crowd shoved them close together—not that Seb minded in the least. Using lack of space as an excuse, he moved behind Andrea and wrapped his arms around him. Only those directly beside them might notice the intimacy of the gesture, and they were too frustrated by the wait to care. To Seb's relief, Andrea uncoiled enough to lean back against him, at least until they stumbled through the turnstile.

By the time they reached the Capri Town station, Andrea had to pry Seb off the window, partly due to the overstuffed car, but mostly because of the spectacular views of the island and the sea beyond. As soon as they broke out into the Piazza Umberto I, Seb made a beeline for the lookout. Andrea caught him by the shirt and veered him down the packed cliffside road. Restaurants hung off the edge like bushels of grapes, the windows of their lower stories reflecting the blues and purples of the sky.

Seb peeked in the first few, full of empty tables. "Not too busy yet."

"Those ones, no."

"Is your aunt's place popular?"

"Number one for midpriced restaurants on Trip Advisor."

Seb whistled. "You don't say."

"It's a smaller place, only forty tables, so she maintains quality. Small staff too, and she owns the building. Everyone tries to poach her chef. Thankfully he's a loyal control freak with not much ambition."

"Better to be king of a small kingdom than knight in a large one."

"*Precisamente.* Also, I'm pretty sure they have a thing going."

"Whatever works." Seb slowed as they approached a pink-washed two-storey building with iron-railed balconies and a faux-marble archway for a door. Slinky black lettering inlaid into the front step announced they'd finally arrived at Fabiana's. "Wow. Okay, tell me again."

"Marilena is my mamma. Though I'm not sure if she will be here. She likes to help out in the kitchen, and Chef Mauro, well…"

"King in his kingdom."

"*Si*. The pregnant lady yelling at everyone to not help her will be my sister, Savina. Just call her Vina. Her husband is Enzo. He'll probably be working the bar. I'm not sure who else is on tonight, but my aunt, of course, is the fabulous Fabiana."

"No uncle?"

To Seb's delight, Andrea dropped his voice to a whisper. "She never married. To this day only she and my mamma know how Bruno came to be. Which explains everything about him. They say the father was a tourist, but…"

"You're worse than a tabloid."

Andrea chuckled. "This is Italy. We invented the paparazzi."

"Any more tea you care to spill before we go in, Hedda Hopper?"

Before Andrea could answer, the lithest and most soignée woman Seb had ever set eyes on floated out to greet them. Swathed in an elegant but curve-hugging blue dress rippling with gemstone winks and glimmers, Fabiana radiated the warmth and welcome of Grace Kelly in her royal era. Her dark hair clipped into a sensible chignon so as not to steal the focus from her long-lashed black eyes, Seb suddenly wanted nothing more than to gaze at her for hours, adoringly. Or maybe keep her portrait in a locket around his neck, the patron saint of all his culinary fantasies.

Instead he took her delicate hand in his, bowed, and kissed it, ignoring Andrea's snort.

"*Zia*, this is my friend Sebastiano."

"Sébastien," he corrected, emphasizing the French pronunciation. "Osaki. From Montreal. An honor."

"Such a charmer you've brought me, Andrea. I like him already."

"The night is young," Andrea teased, finding his smile at last. "How many are we?" Seb didn't miss how he offered his aunt his arm as they strolled into the restaurant, which was, as predicted, empty except for two lingering tables.

The main dining room betrayed the same subtle feminine grace as the lady herself. Wall-to-wall windows showcased the main attraction: the view. The decor, the creamiest of whites and the palest of pinks with silver accents, acted as supporting player. In place of the usual watercolors of local landscapes, sepia-toned pictures of Capri taken by celebrity guests adorned the walls. A wine cellar the size of a walk-in closet enclosed the stairs to the lower-level bar, where tan leather banquettes and animal-skin armchairs complemented the starry late-seventies light fixtures.

A column of framed reviews by the door to the downstairs kitchen caught Seb's eye while Andrea and Fabiana slipped into Chef Mauro's domain. He recognized the names of famous newspaper and magazines critics on most bylines. But the tiniest one, slotted in beside a rave from *GQ* writer Alan Rickman, he remembered from his dog-eared copy of the *Lonely Planet Guide to Naples and the Amalfi Coast* by one Henry Wilson.

Typically Henry captured the swinging atmosphere of Fabiana's and the glamour of the lady herself in two brief but tantalizing paragraphs. Little wonder Seb fell for his writing as much as the man himself. Seb felt that telltale tightening in his chest but fought against it. Part of him wished Henry could be with them tonight, and in this small way, he was. But his sadness settled into a peaceful coexistence with his attraction to and affection for Andrea, who swung back out of the kitchen door, only to stop cold when he spotted Seb.

To his credit, despite the nervousness that thrummed off him like sound waves, Andrea fell in at Seb's side. Waited for him to say something, make a move before freaking out.

"So this is where you met?" Seb asked.

"*Si.*" Seb's gentle hip-check pushed for more. "He cheated a bit because he liked this place so much. He would go to another restaurant early, take a few bites of the food, have a drink—"

"And then come back here for a real dinner. Wasn't the first time, wouldn't be the last."

"Does it bother you?" Andrea asked.

"What? No." Seb leaned his body into Andrea's. "Like you said, I'm not really alone here. Not that I'm not enjoying getting to know new people. But it's nice to have someone familiar around, if only in spirit." Seb counted out a few beats to himself before asking, "Does it bother you that Henry is... well, kind of everywhere?"

Andrea shook his head. "If there's one thing I've learned, Sebastiano, it's that you cannot change the past."

"*Precisamente.*" Seb grinned in the wake of Andrea's laugh.

He slipped a hand into nervy Andrea's as they made their way into the kitchen, not surprised Andrea dropped his when a cry burst out from the far corner. The Sophia Loren to Fabiana's Maria Callas, Marilena Sorrentino exuded that earthy Italian sensuality her son had handsomely inherited.

That was about the only thing he got from her, other than luxurious hair. Where Andrea was fine cut, Marilena was rounded; where he was fit, she was voluptuous. Throughout the evening, Seb would catch an echo of her infectious laugh, belted out of her throat with her head lustily thrown back. She embraced him like one of her own, whispering some Italian wisdom into his ear his soul understood, if not his mind.

Andrea completed the introductions by presenting him to his brother-in-law Enzo, a bear-cuddle man with a furry mustache, and Chef Mauro himself. The maternal gene for wide, lush-lashed black eyes had leapfrogged over Andrea to his sister, Savina, who twiddled her fingers in Seb's direction as she cut little pillows of gnocchi. He tried to figure out if the mischief in her smile qualified as little sister or something more, decided he didn't want to know what that something more might be. Then Fabiana waved them over for instructions as another waiter handed out aprons.

Seb had worn his dove-grey linen pants with a pale-blue dress shirt—not quite the uniform-white shirt with black trousers most waiters wore, but it was the nicest thing he'd brought with him. No one on staff came close to his size, and Fabiana couldn't afford to be picky at the last minute. He'd stuffed a selection of ties in his backpack, but unless the other men waited till the last second to put on their own, they'd stay there. He watched the others spread out. The waiters folded the top edges of their aprons over a few times before fastening them. When Seb attempted to do the same, Andrea snatched his away with a click of his tongue.

"Hey, hey! You are a guest!"

"Don't be ridiculous," Seb chided, tugging his apron back. "I came to help."

He almost laughed at Andrea's outraged look. "No, no, no. Sebastiano—"

"I worked at a sushi stand in a food court for two years in college."

"Oh, really?" Fabiana tutted away any further protests from Andrea. "Where was this?"

"In Vancouver."

"*Bene.* You speak only English?"

"Also French. And Japanese."

"Worldly and charming. Andrea, why haven't you brought this *magnifico* young man to meet me before?"

"I knew what you'd do with him."

She patted Andrea on the cheek. "Ah, *cucciolo*, you know me too well." She turned to address the staff. "Everyone, if any of your tables are more comfortable in French, please have Sébastien second you."

"But you'll keep any tips I make. I'm just here to help."

All the female members of his family shot Andrea a look that said, *See?* He rolled his eyes.

"Now please gather round so Mauro can explain the specials."

A sous chef lined up four steaming plates of food per server, which looked too gorgeous to eat but smelled too enticing to not. Fabiana insisted Seb stand so close beside her he wondered if they would be recreating that scene from *Lady and the Tramp.*

"Don't worry," she whispered, mouth inches from his ear, "I will translate."

"Fabi," Marilena warned in a tone that required no interpretation.

Andrea and Vina poorly swallowed their laughter. No one else dared make a sound.

"I'm sure the food will speak for itself," Seb assured her, tucking in to the first plate.

"Are you sure you want to do this?" Andrea asked for the umpteenth time as he carefully ran his comb through Seb's unruly mane of hair, man-buns being inappropriate for table service and Seb being incapable of fastening a tight ponytail.

The antiseptic smell of the staff bathroom stole the last lingering taste of the specials from his mouth, probably for the best. Seb had to focus on serving the food to other people, not drooling all over their plates. Also, Fabiana had promised to pay him in pasta and torta caprese.

"You need to calm down."

Andrea sighed. "A quiet spot at the bar. You could do some writing."

Seb caught his eye in the mirror. "Is there something you're not saying?"

That spooked him. "No! It's just… You're supposed to be on holiday."

"I am. I'm having fun, with you."

Andrea opened his mouth to reply, settled on a bashful smile. "Okay."

"Are we good now?"

A shrug. He muttered something about "Canadian people" Seb didn't pay much attention to. He gave over to the strokes of the comb, the feel of Andrea's hands gathering and shaping his hair. For all his anxiousness before, Andrea didn't seem to be in too big a rush to tie that ponytail, instead running his fingers through the silken strands.

"Having a moment back there?"

"Mmm." Andrea finally secured the elastic, cinched it with a tug. "It's nice to be on your level for once."

Seb chuckled, tapped the overturned crate Andrea stood on with his ankle. "You enjoying the view?"

"A bit too much."

"Oh?" Seb turned around, took advantage of Andrea's added height to gaze into his eyes. He ran his fingers along the edge of his fresh-shaven jaw—Fabiana liked her waiters groomed and tidy. To that end she had rustled up a uniform for Seb from former staff castoffs. The crisp white shirt hung open at the front; Andrea reached for his top buttons, made to fasten them, but ended up cupping Seb's neck.

Seb thumbed the slight cleft in Andrea's chin, the thick of his bottom lip. Their heavy breaths mingled as they swayed closer together, eager for more of the other's touch. They fell into a slow, sensuous kiss, as if they had all the time in the world to tease and explore. This was, Seb thought, the magic of Andrea: his ability to freeze time, to delay grief and guilt until their moment had passed, washed away by torrents of sensation. Seb pulled their bodies together, massaged his hands up and down Andrea's back until that anxious rigidity softened into tension of a different kind, a tripwire of need begging to be set off.

Someone pounded on the door. They wrenched apart, panting, grinning.

"An-dr-ea!" came Vina's taunting voice. "Zip up your pants and get out here. A busload of Japanese tourists just came through the door."

"*Merda.*" He launched at Seb anew, this time to do up his shirt. "*Andiamo*, Sebastiano."

"Be there in two shakes," Seb shouted at the door. Then to a frazzled Andrea, "Rain check?"

"We'll see."

"We'll see?"

"After a night at Fabiana's, most people are lucky if they can crawl into bed."

"I can do crawling. At least I'll be on my knees."

Andrea let out a flustered breath, shook his head. "What am I going to do with you and your naughty mind?"

"Anything you like." He stole a kiss from Andrea's smirking mouth. "Later."

Seb took a deep, centering breath, then plunged into the fray with Andrea close on his heels. Chef Mauro barked orders at his sous chefs, readying their stations before the first tickets came in. With a wink in their direction, Marilena sang to herself as she put the finishing touches on her mouthwatering desserts. The atmosphere resembled that of a kettle that had just started to percolate, with the occasional burst of steam erupting from different parts of the kitchen.

Vina grabbed Seb before they shot out into the dining room. "Is there anything special we should know?"

"Be professional, not friendly. Serve plates with both hands. Don't touch the food in any way. And if you have some hand towels, preferably cold ones, make a tray and give them out before they start their meal."

She and Andrea nodded. Andrea steered him back to the main dining room, where a group of twenty Japanese tourists waited for the busboys to rearrange the tables for them. Though they appeared unassuming in simple clothes a bit too casual for the restaurant, Seb could tell by their jewelry and gadgets that they came from serious money. Not to mention the Japanese media mogul in their midst. Fabiana conferred with the mogul's personal attaché, who confirmed Seb's suspicion that this was one big, extended family.

He flew into action, bowing deeply to the collective and each of the elders among them. When Fabiana gave him the signal, he introduced himself in Japanese. With a look of relieved amazement, the attaché waved him over and launched into a whispered explanation of their needs. After reassuring the young woman everything would be seen to—and praying it would—he drew Fabiana aside.

"Do you know who that is?" He attempted to point with his eyes since their guests would consider even the slightest gesticulation vulgar.

"Mr. Kawamata," she said. "Is he someone important?"

"He's a senior executive and major shareholder in Fuji Media. More importantly he's a well-known philanthropist and supporter of the arts in Japan. He's here with his entire family for an anniversary trip. But I didn't tell you any of that."

"Of course not."

"In Japan customers don't speak about personal things with wait staff. Don't make a big deal of it or put on the charm. They want professionalism, brisk and efficient service."

"And they will get it." She turned her body, her sly smile just for him. "*Santo Dio* has blessed us tonight, and I am blessed to have you here. I hope Andrea knows how lucky he is."

"With a family like yours, he's the lucky one."

She indulged in a quiet laugh. "Such a charmer."

The next four hours tested not only Seb's language skills but his endurance. Orders and other instructions were relayed to Andrea in Japanese, with Seb hastily scribbling down an English translation at his side, which he would give to Andrea once they were out of sight so as not to shame their guests. Andrea would then translate that into Italian for some of the wait staff and cooks. Discussions or explanations were trickier to navigate. Guests would voice these to the attaché, who would hurry to steal a private moment with Seb.

Unaccustomed to the bustling tempo of a restaurant, Seb struggled to keep pace while pounding up and down the stairs a dozen times a half hour or stay balanced when armed with four meticulously composed plates, all while making like Andrea's shadow, there to learn and serve except when his one special skill was needed, more of a ball chained to his wing-sandaled heel than an angel on his shoulder. By the time they took the dessert orders, Seb felt like he'd rode the entire Tour de France in one go. As Andrea's bicycle.

But all was forgiven when Kawamata-san thanked them

personally for dedicating themselves to their table, a huge honor Seb still reeled from as he swung back into the kitchen.

And barely dodged a tray frisbeed at his head. A skunk-drunk Bruno, doing his best impression of a bull in a china shop, yanked out a utensil drawer and shot the contents across the cooking area floor. Chef Mauro's nimble sous hopped around the sharp objects, never breaking concentration as they continued to churn out plates. Bellowing like an ornery giant despite being shorter than Andrea, Bruno spit in a sauce pot and grabbed for his belt buckle before Andrea intercepted him, shoving him into a corner.

A Vesuvian argument ensued. Marilena charged forward with an accusing finger—two guesses where Andrea got his temper from—and barely avoided getting hit with a wine glass. Seb almost got beaned by the door when Fabiana slipped into the kitchen, hissing for quiet. Seeing the state of her son, she sighed, flicked her fingers at him, and left.

Bruno roared at her dismissal, lobbing glass after glass at the door. Seb scurried over to shield Vina as Andrea attempted to tackle him to the wall. Fury sparked Bruno's fifty-proof blood, and he reared, grabbing one of the glass shards and swiping at his cousin. Andrea jumped back. Bruno raced for the door and the customers beyond.

When he thought about it later, Seb couldn't really explain the impulse to block the exit, standing tall, arms crossed, face granite. Misplaced chivalry? Death wish? Bruno skidded to a stop, snarled. Seb stared him down. He didn't flinch. He didn't glower. He didn't dare him to fight. He just stared, impassive, down into Bruno's bloodshot eyes, repeating his inner mantra: *You shall not pass.*

Bruno shouted at him in Italian, curses and invectives that, perversely, made it easier to ignore him. He got right under Seb's chin with his stinking breath, flecks of spittle spraying his neck. As his volume rose, Bruno's face swelled, purple and sweaty, until he resembled an evil beet. Seb became fascinated with the two inches of roots of his bleached-blond undercut hair, marveling at how some people actively worked against their own attractiveness. He suppressed a yawn as Bruno continued to spew his bile and, if his gestures were anything to go by, homophobic filth. Seb was the anvil, and he was the relentless hammer. But Seb had customers waiting, not to mention the smell was getting to him, so he searched for an endgame.

Bruno punched him point-blank in the stomach. Once, twice, a few wild jabs; Seb stumbled, grappling for a wall to avoid falling on the shattered glass. Bruno spat on his head, tried to dart past him, but Seb kicked out his leg and tripped him. That one judo class his father forced him into finally paid off. Bruno toppled into the no-longer-so-cuddly arms of Enzo, who grabbed him by the scuff of his neck and threw him into the supply closet like a rabid cub.

Breathing rapidly through his nose, Seb struggled not to vomit up all those specials. It felt as if his diaphragm cowered under his rib cage and his stomach had gone ten rounds with a meat tenderizer. His chest ached, cinching in his lungs whenever he tried to draw in an extra dose of much-needed oxygen. A pair of gentle hands helped ease him over to a stool. For several minutes his entire world winnowed down to inhaling, exhaling, clenching through a spasm of pain.

Someone—Vina—brought him a cold glass of water. Seb managed a few sips; the acid searing up his throat retreated. Slowly he forced himself to relax, found more space in his lungs. The world around him came crashing back: Bruno scratching at the supply closet door like a cat in a bag; Andrea berating himself in a corner, still shaking with fury; Vina stroking Seb's back as Enzo prepared an ice pack; Marilena muttering as she swept up the glass.

"Just another boring night at Fabiana's," Seb rasped out, if only to hear Vina laugh.

"Andrea!" His sister unleashed a blast of Italian that smote the last of his ire.

He spun around, gasped, and sped over to Seb's side.

"Ay, Sebastiano…"

"My own fault. I shouldn't have gotten in his way."

"Don't be stupid." Vina tapped the back of his head in a way that would have been a slap if he'd felt better. "He would have terrorized the guests. *Dio* knows what might have happened. You saved our customers and our reputation. I'm sure my aunt will agree, if she ever decides to clean up her own mess."

Seb expected at least a cursory protest from Andrea, but he preoccupied himself with examining Seb's middle.

"Do you mind?" he asked, grabbing the slack in his shirt.

"Go for it," Seb agreed, wishing it were under sexier circumstances.

Andrea winced at the bruises that already bloomed on Seb's navel. His cautious prods didn't do much to pluck out the stitches that cramped Seb's front and left side.

"Nothing is broken, but I would like to call a doctor."

"You are a doctor. Do you really think there's a chance of internal bleeding? He didn't hit me that hard."

"I think I've taken enough chances where you are concerned, Sebastiano."

Before Seb could answer that, Fabiana swanned in.

"Mr. Kawamata's assistant is asking about the desserts. What should I tell him?" Seb grit his teeth through the pain of holding Andrea down. Fabiana gasped, having finally got a good look at Seb. "*O Santo Dio!* Are you hurt?"

Seb didn't think he was the only one wondering if she was more concerned about his ability to serve the rest of the meal than his health. He began to sympathize a bit with Bruno, seeing this snapshot of his life.

"Someone will have to carry the trays, but I can finish the table." He shushed Andrea's protest before it left his lips. "I'll just need a minute or two. Can you offer them a digestif?"

"Ah! What a treasure you are!" Fabiana pinched his cheek. "Pity you don't live closer. You could be here every night!"

With that she fluttered off, a pretty cloud onto which you could project shapes and shadows, of no more substance than air. The three of them—himself, Andrea, and Vina—gaped at each other, then burst out laughing.

Better that than crying over broken glasses and spoilt sauce, Seb thought.

Chapter Ten

GLIMPSES OF DARK HAIR,
MAHOGANY SKIN AMIDST
THE BILLOWS OF STEAM
-#173, *IN BLUE SOLITUDES*, S. WILSON-OSAKI

A glutton's moon hung over Capri when they finally escaped Fabiana's. The scent of palm and wisteria lured them along the posh Via Federico Serena, lined with luxury shops whose displays spotlighted a level of glamour beyond their reach. The sky and sea beyond, the lustrous blue of a sapphire, enchanted Seb far more than any Armani or Zegna suit, though he wouldn't have minded seeing Andrea in something bespoke, and said so.

Vina snorted so hard Seb thought she might trip. A soft chuckle from under his shoulder signaled the man himself was amused but noncommittal. Or possibly just exhausted. Once Kawamata-san's party had left to hit the clubs, an implacable Andrea forced Seb to hang up his apron, then bundled him into one of the bar's plush armchairs with a pot of tea and a sliver of torta caprese. Seb's sidelining meant Andrea had to pick up his slack until Fabiana dismissed them around 1:30 a.m., once Bruno had been carted off to the drunk tank.

Though his gut still ached, having a warm, sleepy-eyed Andrea glued to his side worked a treat, mostly on Seb's libido. He hadn't been briefed on their destination, but he hoped it involved a working coffee machine so he could caffeinate some desire into Andrea, who dozed on Seb's shoulder as they strolled. Given Andrea had been awake for nearly twenty-four hours, Seb should have been more considerate. But they had worked hard, and now he wanted to play hard. They needed to vent some of the high emotion of the day, preferably all over each other.

Vina glanced back at them for the third time, her sphinxlike smile too tightly encrypted for the caveman state of Seb's brain to decipher. She and Enzo swung their clasped hands in time with the noxious electronic beat blaring out of a passing bar, her pregnancy too advanced for them to couple up.

Just when Seb expected them to veer down one of the side streets, they continued toward the main entrance to the Grand Hotel Quisisana, a five-star palace of Doric columns and crystal chandeliers. Ladies draped in jewels that cost more than his house and their portly, Rolexed companions lounged around wicker and white outdoor tables. A gilt but welcoming light glowed out of the reception area, which, to Seb's shock, Vina and Enzo sauntered into, waving at the night manager.

Seb hoped he hadn't just walked into a John le Carré novel.

"Uh… what are we doing here?" he whispered as they passed a statue clutching a toga to her chest despite a peak-a-boo breast.

"Enzo is the head concierge," Vina supplied. "We live on the grounds."

They crossed straight through to the rear patio, then into the gardens. A serpentine path through the palm trees and manicured shrubs led to a gated staircase on the far side of the infinity pool. A series of cute but less-fancy bungalows bordered the lower ledge, their linked back terraces looking out to sea. When they reached the third one, Enzo proffered a set of keys.

"Lucky for you, my colleague is on holiday. You have the place all to yourselves."

"People go on holiday when they live here?" Seb asked, incredulous.

A shrug was all the answer he got.

"We're over here. The balconies in the back all connect. Come over when you want breakfast."

"Or lunch," Vina added, a twinkle in her eye.

"Thank you." Seb struggled to form words that expressed his appreciation. "For everything."

"Just make sure he gets some sleep." Vina's black eyes shone with affection for her brother. "He works too hard."

"I'll take good care of him."

Finally Seb earned a genuine smile. "I know you will."

Seb watched them slip into the shadow of the far door, then all but carried his snoozing charge into their private bungalow. He flicked on the lights to reveal a simple but cozy open-concept room with a view most people would donate a kidney for. He waddled them over to the bed, wondering if he should wrap Andrea in the fluffy duvet and jerk off in the shower, when a pair of callused hands began to explore. Specifically his lower posterior region. Seb plunked his backpack by the nightstand and shifted Andrea into a full-body embrace.

"I thought you were down for the count."

"Mmm-mmm. What's the word? Power napping." Andrea meticulously mapped the curve of his buttocks before moving front to, alas, play doctor. And not the good kind. "How are you feeling?"

"Go back to what you were doing, and I'll be just fine."

A throaty chuckle made Seb's groin throb. "Give me an honest answer, and I'm yours."

"It's still a bit raw, but I'll survive."

"*Bene.*" Andrea snaked his arms around Seb's back, closing the distance between them. His lean, wiry body coiled with tension, the press of his hips sparking Seb's thrumming need to life. Andrea took his mouth with surprising fervor, his kiss decadent and devouring. "All night I thought only of this. Only of being here with you." His low, frantic moans and the insistent prod of his erection begged Seb to command him.

He didn't have to ask twice. Breaking their kiss, Seb pushed him back a step. Took a moment to admire the panting, red-lipped mess of him, hair wild, eyes burning, shirt rumpled, pants tented. A lion in heat.

"Shower."

A smirk of approval twisted his lips. Andrea led him to a spacious bathroom of dark-hued ceramic tiles and golden fixtures. A glass wall partitioned off the generous shower stall, with a back bench that gave Seb ideas. Throwing a bath mat over the bidet, he ordered Andrea to sit. The balance of the position forced his full-mast prick against the seam of his tight trousers. Andrea half swallowed a grunt, clamped his hands on his knees. Seb watched as he worked through the sensation, as he harnessed his breathing and returned his full attention to Seb.

For which he would be richly rewarded. Seb stood before him, letting Andrea's avid gaze reach for him everywhere he longed to touch, then slowly plucked open a shirt cuff. He ran his fingers over his sensitive wrist, tracing patterns as he imagined Andrea would do if he caressed him there. When he heard the click of Andrea's throat, he moved to his collar, lazily popping one button, another, and another, exposing his chest. A sharp intake of breath added final punctuation to the run-on stripping of Seb's shirt. He got a little raunchy when he unlatched his belt buckle—what gay man wouldn't channel *Magic Mike*?—whipping it at Andrea, who tried and failed to catch it with his teeth.

Laughing, Seb slowly unzipped to reveal the bulge in his boxers. Andrea smacked his lips, a flick of tongue luring him forward. Seb swaggered over, rubbed his silk-clad shaft into Andrea's cheek. A purring groan reverberated through his balls. Andrea's heavy breaths steamed through the dense fabric, stoking his already turgid shaft. Time to chug along before this train left the station too early.

Seb tapped Andrea's chin up. He pulled out the tie in his hair, letting it fan out over his bare shoulders. Andrea gulped, hands white-knuckling his knees. Hovering a moment, Seb stared into his gray-green eyes until they went deep-sea dark, until Andrea chafed against his self-imposed reins. Only then did Seb kick out of his pants, snap the elastic waist of his boxers before easing them down over his proud, ready cock. He cranked on the shower to warm the water, then motioned for Andrea to stand.

He made quick business of stripping him, relishing how Andrea shivered, shook, even whined a bit when Seb left unzipping his trousers to the very last. As fun as their little game was, Seb kept him covered because the scent of him was maddening. Musky and familiar, the smell of a favorite leather jacket, sweat stained but so comfortable. Seb cupped his face to keep from groping lower, dragged a thumb over his opulent bottom lip. Andrea suckled it greedily, demonstrating in miniature just how skilled his tongue was.

Seb almost, almost—so close—ordered him to his knees.

"Do you want me now?" he asked, unable to pry his eyes or his thumb from that talented mouth. "Or do you want to wash me?"

A small gasp. Andrea shut his eyes, let him slip out. The violence of his full-body quake had Seb worried he'd pushed him over the edge. Andrea drank in a deep breath, calmed, but just.

"How do you know?" He shook his head, but didn't seem to clear it. "What I like, how to... How do you know what to do to me?"

"A magician never reveals his—"

"*Bastardo.*"

"Excuse me?"

Andrea let out a grunt that seemed to crawl up from his bowels, sucking in another deep breath. "I would, yes. To wash you, yes, please."

"And then? What would you like? For me to fuck you?" A hiss. "To bend you over that bench and fuck you?"

A rip of pleasure threatened to peel off a layer of Andrea's skin, but he held on.

"*Magari*. But..."

"Hmm?"

His hesitation almost undid Seb, it was so delicious. "Against the wall. Under the water."

"Mmm. We'll see."

Seb offered him his hand. Andrea took it and more, smashing them together and scorching his mouth with a kiss. Seb matched his fire and his ferocity until their hips fell into an all-too-tempting rhythm. Greedy himself, he didn't want this to end. They had only so many tomorrows, none guaranteed. But before he could decide on a move, Andrea broke off, bowing his head even as he gasped for breath.

Seb lifted his chin, ghosted a kiss over his lips. He held the door for Andrea as they entered the shower stall. Andrea melted into the water as if he needed it to breathe. Seb tore away from that sensual visual long enough to fetch them some supplies—condoms, lube, and a washcloth. But as soon as he shut the shower door behind him, the steam billowed around them, and they crossed into another, private dimension.

Andrea grabbed him, swapped places. Guided Seb's head under the jets to soak his hair and followed the stream down his torso with tender fingers, then spun him around. Seb shut his eyes, concentrated on the tub-thump of his pulse in his ears. Opened his other senses to this singular experience.

A fresh herby scent infused the humid air. Andrea started at the base of his neck, massaging the washcloth over his skin with the same gentleness with which he'd tended to Federica. But Seb wasn't a distressed horse. He reared into Andrea's touch, encouraging him to scrub. Andrea chuckled but increased the pressure, getting especially frisky on Seb's buttocks and inner thighs. A vigorous swipe to his perineum had Seb panting; a thorough fondle of his balls had him cursing in both of Canada's official languages.

By the time Andrea eased him around to work on his front—conveniently from his knees—the showerhead wasn't the only thing dripping profusely. Squinting to keep his eyes shut, Seb couldn't help but reach for Andrea's shoulders. Between the muscles undulating beneath that supple skin, the washcloth lighting up every nerve end it brushed, and the whispers of proximity that prickled up the length of Seb's sin-hard cock, the current of sensual excitement threatened to sweep him away. Then Andrea moved to his chest, and Seb bit his tongue to keep from coming.

After foaming up a generous lather, both on the cloth and between them, Andrea dabbed his collar, paying extra attention to his suprasternal notch. Seb cursed when Andrea flicked the corner over a tight-puckered nipple, crooned when he worried his aureole in a circular motion. Andrea pushed in so close that barely an inch separated them. He dragged the cloth down Seb's navel but stopped just above the slick head of his cock. The merest gyration could escalate their interlude to the highest level. But Seb waited, kneading Andrea's shoulders and neck, twining his fingers in the black whorls of his hair.

Andrea tossed the cloth aside. Pressing their foreheads together, Seb eased him under the spray. Locked in on Andrea's dark eyes as the water poured over them. Stole a wet, ravenous kiss before they crashed together. Laughing, fumbling, moaning till they found the perfect spot, Andrea spread-eagled against the back wall, half-kneeling on the bench. Seb suited up away from the clouds of steam, eye fucking Andrea's pert, perfect backside, ripe for plunder. He canted the showerhead to cascade over them, his breaths short and frantic. His cock pulsed in anticipation of the pound, of plunging into the body that submitted so completely to him.

Andrea summoned him back with a growl, not so meek after all. He bucked his hips into Seb's groin when he finally saddled up, his thick-swollen cock leaking fat drops of precome onto the bench. Seb had planned to tease out preparing him, but his caveman brain howled with want. He started with two double-lubed fingers and finished with the head of his cock. Andrea opened so effortlessly for him, snorting with bullish intensity as Seb sheathed himself.

Seb abandoned himself to the rhythm, to the heat, to the grunt and the sweat and the deep, deep, deep bliss of reigning over another man. He lasted longer than he thought he would, his body craving the fevered communion more than the quake of completion. He climbed onto the bench, cradling Andrea so he could thrust deeper, craning his head back to suck his tongue. Palmed him and pumped until he keened into Seb's mouth. Slammed his pleasure-wrecked body against the wall as Seb's flooded with ecstasy, bursting out of him with a fizzy champagne afterglow.

They cocooned there, panting, snickering until Andrea's head lolled onto Seb's chest and he felt him go slack. Seb let him sleep, carrying him first out of the shower to towel him off—more or less—then into bed. The sheets would dry. Seb shut off the water and sank in beside Andrea, already curled into a little spoon. Tucking in behind him, Seb drank in the smell of his damp hair as he drifted off to sleep: the scent of Italy, the scent of rejuvenation, the scent of life.

A warm, cinnamony aroma lured Seb back into the land of the living. He flopped onto his back, waiting for sunlight to pink his eyelids, but they remained dark. Keeping his eyes shut, he listened for the sandpaper rasp of Henry's breathing. Fully awake thanks to the unfamiliar room around him, Seb sent out a five-fingered search party, found the bed beside him empty. Clammy but empty.

It came back to him as it always did—the sharp slap of realization—but it didn't bite as normal, the permafrost spreading farther over his heart. Instead a fault line had cracked that chill surface. Several, in fact. A second name skated through his still-groggy brain, performing triple loops and double axels to get his attention. Andrea, who brought the sunshine.

Seb lazed there awhile longer, reliving the night before. The restaurant, their shower interlude, but also being woken in the night by Andrea's deft tongue on his cock. Too recently for Seb's slack member to take much notice now. He blinked his eyes open but saw no sign of Andrea in the cottage bedroom. The balcony door shut tight and the blind drawn so only a thin crease of light shimmered through, Seb wondered if Andrea had decamped for Vina and Enzo's, or whether he had returned to the mainland. Worry eluded him, part of his new, embrace-what-life-throws-at-you attitude. If Andrea didn't leave a message, then that was a message in and of itself.

He hoisted himself into a sitting position, his abdomen screaming. Pulling the covers back revealed Bruno's fist had painted a garish tattoo across his midsection in prizefighter purples, meat-locker blues, and puke yellows. After a pit stop in the bathroom to slowly—very slowly—freshen up, Seb dug a pair of shorts and his best T-shirt out of his backpack, then set off in search of an espresso. Not to mention his love-'em-and-leave-'em bed partner.

He heard the argument as soon as he cracked open the balcony door. The rat-tat-tat of Italian voices—first Andrea's, then Vina's—sprayed the placid morning with verbal gunfire. Seb eased the door open just enough to peer out without being seen. Vina stood her ground, arms crossed over her growing belly, as Andrea enacted a tempestuous pantomime of angry poses. As if a director fed him lines, every comment she made sent him flailing into ever more vehement paroxysms.

Then all at once, Andrea froze, sagged. Waved his hands in an impotent gesture and retreated to the balcony rail. Vina moved to join him. Andrea bowed his head as if suddenly defeated; she rubbed his back. Seb ignored the tight feeling in his chest, reminding himself whatever was going on was none of his business. The siblings whispered together for a while, Vina seeming to encourage her brother. In what, Seb could only guess, but he wagered Bruno was involved somehow.

He waited a few more minutes until Andrea had straightened a bit. Seb rattled the door and let out a loud yawn before venturing onto the balcony, to be greeted by a pair of bemused faces.

"*Buongiorno a tutti*," he declared, trying not to lurch too much and alert Andrea to the ache in his abs. He made a poor show of it because Dr. Sorrentino was instantly on the case, rushing over to poke at his side.

"Ah, Sebastiano." A crease already marred his brow. "How are you feeling?"

"In dire need of some liquid therapy."

Vina laughed. "I'll get your espresso."

"You are a goddess."

She scoffed. "*Zia* Fabi was right about you."

Seb waited until she'd waddled into the house before greeting Andrea properly. Plush lips welcomed him with an eagerness they could not indulge for too long, but Seb wasn't complaining.

"What was that about?" Seb asked, pulling away before the urge to drag Andrea back to their cottage and fuck him legless took over.

Andrea exhaled a blustery breath. "Later."

"Your cousin up to more tricks?"

"Pfft! Forget about him." He laced their hands to lead him over to a wrought-iron table set for four. "We have bigger problems."

Seb raised his eyebrows. "Such as?"

"Mamma has invited us for dinner tonight."

Unable to keep from snickering at Andrea's look of annoyance, he waited a few beats before answering. "I would love to go to your mom's."

A sigh. "That is what I thought you would say."

"You don't want to go? It is Sunday night. It's tradition."

He perked up a bit at this. "In Japanese families too?"

"I'm half-French, remember?"

"*Si, si.*" He appeared to struggle to order his thoughts, so Seb gave him some space, walking over to the rail. Capri in the morning—playground of the gods. After a minute Andrea fell in beside him. "Normally I would go. But it would be the second night in a row you spend with my family, and…"

"You want me all to yourself?" He didn't get his laugh. Instead Andrea's downcast eyes were back, along with a faint blush. "What is it?"

"When do you leave?"

Seb stared at Andrea—the loyal, giving, indefatigable lover he hadn't asked for but was infinitely grateful he'd found—and wondered when things had veered into the serious. Both this conversation and the formless something between them, far from solid yet but growing denser every day. They both knew the limits of their time together, but a night like the one they just shared could blur the sharpest of lines. Maybe Andrea was setting up boundaries. Seb considered delineating some of his own, as he was in no position, emotionally or otherwise, to offer more than a few weeks' dalliance.

"Wednesday."

Seb hoped Andrea's nod was one of acceptance. "*Bene*. Then there is time."

"Not to Canada just yet. To Sorrento for a few days." The words were out before Seb really thought them through. But they felt right, which freaked him out. "Halfway to the airport. You're welcome any night you want to stop in."

To Seb's relief, Andrea brightened. "How long are you there?"

"Until next Sunday."

Andrea nodded, thinking. "Tell me honestly, Sebastiano. What do you want to do tonight?"

Seb leaned in to whisper, "Take you back to my place and lick you from head to toe." At Andrea's shiver, he added, "After having what will probably be the best dinner of my trip at your mamma's."

Andrea rolled his eyes. "Fabiana *is* right about you."

"We should invite the ladies. If your mom doesn't mind. I have a feeling they'll get along."

At that the clouds parted from Andrea's solemn visage to make way for a dazzling smile. "And if we happen to disappear while they're entertaining her…"

"So be it." Which earned his ass a pinch.

"I like the way your mind works."

Seb hip-checked him. "Just my mind?"

"While we are on my sister's balcony, yes."

As if waiting for their cue, Enzo and Vina exited their cottage, the former with a massive tray laden with every breakfast delight one could ask for: eggs two ways, a heaping plate of bacon and sausage, toast, crêpes, yogurt, a bowl of fresh fruit, and a basket of pastries. Seb suspected he'd snatched it from the hotel. Vina served espressos and blood orange juice mimosas—an impossible choice if ever there was one.

Once everyone sat down, Seb raised his glass.

"A toast." Seb took a moment to drink everything in— peerless view, enchanting company—then said, "To my new lovely friends and to... second chapters in life."

They cheered, clinked glasses. Seb couldn't help but meet Andrea's thoughtful gaze across the table, inwardly vowing to do everything in his power to brighten him up over the next few days.

"So what do you have planned for today, Sebastiano?" Vina asked. Andrea's nickname for him was spreading.

"Don't answer that," Andrea warned.

Seb laughed. "Why? Is Fabiana expecting another party of Japanese tourists?"

"Don't joke about that either."

Around his mouthful of toast, Enzo said to Andrea, "She already asked for you."

"She asks too much." Vina sighed. "We said no. We didn't want to wake you for that. I hope that's okay."

"You mean you didn't dare." Seb put on his wickedest smirk.

Vina shrugged. "Nothing I haven't walked in on before, believe me."

"Oh-ho!" Seb admired Andrea's blush. "Have a bit of an exhibitionist streak, do we, Dre?"

"Just a sister who doesn't knock."

"We all have one of those," Seb commiserated.

But Enzo trumped them. "Some of us have three."

"And you'd all be lost without us," Vina huffed, stealing one of his sausages. "And enough of changing the subject. Sebastiano?"

"No particular plans." Seb sliced into a peach so juicy he let it drip into his mimosa. "I'm here in Capri. Might as well take a look around."

She nodded. "Andrea will show you the best places."

A soft curse from the other side of the table heralded a sharp exchange in Italian between the siblings. Seb managed to pick out a few words, none of which he liked.

"I know he has to work." Seb attempted to silence the bickering. "We're seeing each other tonight."

Vina dismissed this with a wave despite her brother's continued protests. "Enzo will drive Andrea's clients today. And because you, Sebastiano, were so generous last night, he has no reason to complain that he finally has a day off."

Something in what she said caught Andrea up short. "What do you mean, 'generous'?"

Seb opened his mouth to object but knew it was pointless. He'd have better luck convincing the moon not to rise than swaying Vina from whatever path she blazed down.

"Your *amante* insisted that his salary and tips be divided between the regular staff. Even the enormous tip the Japanese *padrino* left him." She continued on in Italian, but Andrea had tuned her out. He shook his head in dismay, but his eyes had regained their luster, shining in a way that made Seb's stomach do a little flip. "I know you would not cancel on your clients at the last minute, so Enzo will take care of them, and you and Sebastiano can spend the day together." She grabbed Seb by the hand, squeezing so hard he thought he heard a snap. "Promise me, *per favore*, that you will not let him talk or think about work. Or answer his phone when one of those—"

"*Basta.*" Enzo shushed his wife with a bearish rumble. "It's all arranged. Let's enjoy our breakfast."

Seb winked at Vina. He had his standing orders for the day and would do his darndest to accomplish his mission: fun.

Chapter Eleven

FORGOTTEN PATHS WIND
DOWN TO A TRUNCATED BEACH,
CRAVING THE OCEAN'S KISS
-#83, *In Blue Solitudes*, S. WILSON-OSAKI

The purr of the motorbike reverberated through Seb's body from ten feet away, revving up all of his senses and… other urges. Andrea straddled the testy beast with the cool of a bull rider, the sparkle off the chrome detailing glinting in his mirror sunglasses. He petted the up-slope of leather seat behind him, and Seb's cock gave a restless twitch. He took a mental pic of Andrea astride that all-day foreplay machine, then swung on behind him.

Andrea's citrusy pomade elevated the ride down the lemon tree-lined hill to a scratch-and-sniff experience. Arms laced around Andrea's middle and helmet free, Seb closed his eyes to better feel the rush of air flapping the sides of his baggy T-shirt. He quickly learned to lean into Andrea and the curve as they navigated the twisty, crowded side streets. The hum of the engine, a lulling constant that reminded Seb he hadn't had enough sleep, distracted him from the view until they zipped out of Capri Town.

Nothing in the world could dim the magnificence of this jewel isle. Lush flora and shrubby trees sprouted from the mountainous landscape. Aquamarine waters tantalized from the base of every dead-drop cliff. Seb whooped and hollered as they climbed toward Anacapri, his fingers itching to scrawl his every thought, impression, idea about this rapturous place onto the pages of his journal. Instead he hugged tight to Andrea and focused on living it.

After a quick zip around the town, they parked by the chairlift to the summit of Mount Solaro, the highest point on Capri. Seb eyed the single-person chairlift skeptically, wondering how many people died each year by accidentally tipping out of the flimsy contraption. Two flirty Italian broncos helped people onto the chairs as quick and casual as short-order cooks flipping burgers, giving pert-bunned girls an extra pat or two. Seb had to remind himself three times to do what Henry would do before heeding Andrea's whistle from the ticket booth.

"Single or return, Sebastiano?"

"Is there a way down?"

"*Si*, by foot."

"Return." He caught Andrea's subtle shake of his head. "You know how I feel about stairs. Besides, I want to see as much of the island as I can."

"We shouldn't rush. You can come back another day to see the rest."

"But I won't be with you." He brushed up against Andrea's backside as he slunk off to get them *granite al limone* at a local café, glancing back in time to catch Andrea's shocked but pleased expression.

Several slurps of tart, tingly goodness later, Seb felt better equipped to brave the chairlift. As they moved toward the front of the line and he noticed just how far above the adjacent valley the lift soared, he began to wish his *granita* were spiked. With a bucket of gin.

"Scared of heights?" Andrea queried with a slight frown. "We can do something else."

"I'll be fine once I get up there. I don't mind the looking. It's the hanging from a few bars of rusted steel and a barely there wicker seat that... well." Gin and vodka *and* rum, for good measure.

Before Andrea could reply, the woman in front of them moved into position. Andrea stroked a calming touch down his back, nudged him forward. Seb stepped into the next chair's path, squinting against the glare of the midday sun. His heart pounded in his ears. Time slowed with every twinge of trepidation. It felt like an eternity before two strong arms braced him for impact, guided him onto the seat, and pinched him on the ass before he flew into the ether.

Seb spun around to give one of the broncos the stink eye, met Andrea's laughing face. Made a crude come-on gesture once they were in the air. Andrea grabbed his crotch as if to say, *You want this?* Seb smirked, winked.

Who was he kidding? He did.

Fifteen minutes later Seb peered over the edge of the rail at the sprinkling of white boats anchored in the azure waters of the Gulf of Naples. Bushels of buttercup-yellow flowers garlanded the observation area while a few threadbare, almost coniferous trees provided a little shade. A corroded statue of Emperor Augustus proudly waved them toward his dominion, specifically the Faraglioni at the far end of the island, three stacked rock formations that jutted out of the sea like crocodile's teeth.

"I come all the way to Italy, only to be reminded of Quebec." Seb laughed as he fiddled with his smartphone. He pulled up a photo of Percé Rock off the Gaspé Peninsula to show Andrea. "This is a big tourist attraction off our southeastern shore."

Andrea compared the photo of a long slab of rock with an archway pierced into its right flank to the toothsome stacks in the distance.

"Perhaps the Faraglioni were cut out of Percé when the continents divided. Italy and Quebec are like… twins separated at birth."

"That's a romantic notion," Seb teased.

Which earned him a shrug, this time a bit sheepish. "I have been accused of worse."

Seb leaned over to swipe at his phone, bringing up a 1980s-era photo of his family posing in front of Percé Rock. Three-year-old him sported a bowl cut with matching sailor-style shirt and shorts. He always got a kick out of his mom's big sunglasses, bigger hair, and enormous pregnant belly. His dad had actually cracked a smile, so it must have been a really good day.

"One of our first family trips." He felt Andrea shudder against his side as he fought not to laugh. "My father was still pretty new to Canada, and poor, back then, so most holidays were spent showing him around the province and hitting the usual French-Canadian haunts, like Old Orchard and Fort Lauderdale."

"Those are where?"

"Maine and Florida. Near Miami."

"Ah, Miami! I've always wanted to go."

Seb nodded. "It's a fun place, but I prefer the Keys."

Andrea indulged in a soft chuckle. "You look so…"

"Stereotypical?"

"Cute."

"Very diplomatic."

"They are a beautiful couple." He handed the phone back but kept hold of Seb by hooking an arm around his waist. "Are you… close?"

"Their relationship didn't last much longer than that picture." Seb tucked his phone in his pocket, glanced around to see if anyone might take a snap of the two of them. This was the first memory in a long time he wanted to keep. "My dad isn't the most… forthcoming person. His work involves a lot of secrecy, and that bleeds into his life. My mom says that in the beginning, when he first came to Canada as a student, he was excited for the opportunity and for the adventure. I don't think he was expecting to settle down so quickly. But he met my mom, and, well… boom."

Andrea grinned. "You mom is very boom."

"Right? So he did the man thing where he thought with his dick for, I guess, seven years. Or he eventually lost his love goggles. I mean, it's not like we've ever talked about it. But my dad's always been about responsibility, and once he started working and they had a bit of money… My mom is more boho, classic French laissez-faire. I guess the excitement of being somewhere new and with someone so different just wore off. He took us back to Japan when I was five and, yeah... I don't think he realized how homesick he was. I don't know what went down, just that, after the month was up, we went home and he stayed."

Andrea hissed in a breath. "*Ohimè*."

"The official reason was work, but not even five-year-old me believed that. He continued to support us and stayed in contact, but he didn't come back to Canada for a few years. And they divorced, obviously. He eventually moved out to Vancouver, as always for 'work,' with his new wife and my half-brother. I went through a rough patch with my mom at the end of high school, so I moved out there for university. Kind of wanted to reconnect with him. But he was so conservative. Any sense of adventure he had died that day we landed in Tokyo."

"How does he feel about..." Andrea made a vague gesture at their twined forms.

Seb let out a bitter laugh. "Well, I met Henry while I was in Vancouver. Not that he was my first boyfriend... To be honest, my dad and I don't speak much, but I feel like that has more to do with my job. Being an editor/translator isn't an important enough career for his firstborn son. The irony being that I minored in Japanese to feel closer to him and that side of myself. He's never said anything about my sexuality, but then we don't exactly have heart-to-hearts. The last time I saw him smile was when I invited him to my wedding. Until he found out it was to a man. He didn't come, but he did buy me a present: a single plane ticket to Japan."

Andrea grunted. "He wanted you to go to Tokyo and

what?"

"Find myself a wife. Probably still does. So here I am. In Amalfi." They snickered. "Or, well, Capri. My mom and I are good. She lives near Quebec City with her boyfriend now, so I don't see her much. Makes sense that she prefers to be close to her grandkids."

That earlier solemnity seemed to infect Andrea anew.

"So when you go back, you'll really be alone."

Seb gave him a playful shove, hoping to knock the seriousness out.

"I have friends, you know. And…" He paused for dramatic effect, shifting around so he could see Andrea's reaction. "… a cat."

"You have a cat?! Why didn't you tell me?"

"I got the feeling you were more of a dog person, and I didn't want to ruin your image of me."

The return of Andrea's smile relieved Seb.

"I am an *animal* person. Tell me about this fortunate creature."

"Her name is Nagiko. She's… Here." He proffered a picture of his little feline snowball. Andrea's resulting "Ay!" went straight to his heart. "She's a little hunter. Loves to be outside, even in winter. Flipside of that is we don't have any mice. She's with the neighbor right now. Her kids love her so much I suspect I might not get her back. But we have adjoining properties, so she's always over there, anyway."

"Perfect for sharing custody."

"Exactly."

"She reminds me of you."

"Probably why she always liked Henry best." Seb

frowned. "Sorry. I shouldn't talk about him so much."

"I would be worried if you didn't. He was your life."

Seb steeled against the bite of those words, found the fangs of heartache didn't cut as deep as they normally would. He still missed Henry, still wished he were there, but with the pair of them. Henry would have loved Andrea—had opened up to him once upon a time, steering him down a path that, unbeknownst to him, led straight to Seb. The symmetry took Seb's breath away.

"He is. And will always be. But it's time to make new memories."

He snatched back his phone and flicked on the camera, tugging Andrea over to the rail so they could pose together, the ancient crags of the Faraglioni completing their postcard-ready pic.

They caught a very late-afternoon ferry by the skin of their teeth after hopping the line for the funicular just as the doors to the last car closed. The attendant, an old friend—and by his envious look, a former flame of Andrea's—clicked his tongue but didn't detain them. Seb outpaced Andrea as they raced down the docks. Stairs he struggled with, but he excelled at all-out sprints. They hit the upstairs bar seconds after the ship launched, downing two waters each before buying out their meager stock of gin and tonic. Never too early to start the party, as Seb had learned from the ladies, who were probably slurping down their predinner cocktails at that very moment.

Commandeering the last two seats by the port-side rail, Andrea propped up his feet as Seb played bartender. A day of fun and relaxation had smoothed the creases from Andrea's brow. Though they had packed a lot into only a few hours, Seb never felt rushed. Whether strolling through the picturesque gardens of Villa San Michele, picnicking in the Giardini di Augusto, or touring the library and exhibitions at the Certosa di San Giacomo, showing off the island had helped to resurrect Andrea's spirit.

This time together also transformed Seb's holiday fling into a genuine friendship. From their banter and teasing to more heartfelt conversations, Seb went from seeing a detailed sketch of a man to a full, complex portrait—filled in with colors vibrant and somber. Seb admired them all. As he sipped his G&T and stretched out beside Andrea to watch the sun set, Seb realized this had been his first 100 percent happy day since a drunk driver ended his world three years ago. The first of many more, he promised himself.

Andrea's phone buzzed, ruining the moment.

"Don't answer that."

Andrea glanced at the screen, tensed. "It's Renia."

Seb tried to pick out as many French-similar words in the ensuing conversation as he could, worried about the health of Federica's twins slightly more than their plans for the evening. He doubted a truckload of pigeons hitchhiked to the symphony, so he shifted his concentration to reading Andrea's expression. The results were… odd. Not yet an expert in the nuances of even that handsome face, Seb thought he saw bewilderment with a side order of shock. By the time Andrea slid his phone in his back pocket, the suspense was killing him.

And continued to torment him. Andrea tucked in beside him, poured another G&T, and stared out at the coastline with an air of befuddlement.

"So? Are the foals okay? Is something wrong with Federica?" Seb waited exactly thirty seconds before making his demands.

"What? Oh, yes, everyone is fine."

"Then what's that look on your face?"

"My…" Andrea blinked rapidly, self-conscious. "It seems that word of the twins has spread to the neighbors."

"No surprise there."

"True." Andrea seemed to be playing the conversation back in his mind. "Someone close by has a sister who is a journalist, and she wants to interview me tomorrow."

"About the twins?"

"*Sì.*"

"That's amazing!"

"Well, it's… something."

His muted response baffled Seb. "Are you camera shy? You look more spooked than a horse."

"No, no. I've been interviewed for the news before. When my father died." Andrea appeared to search the sunset sky for answers. "But this will draw attention."

"To the fact that you don't have a practice? Is what you did illegal?"

Andrea shook his head. "I have a license. I mean, the local guys won't be happy about it, but if their paycheck means more than the animals they care for, well…"

"You reap what you sow." Seb considered the broader implications. "But this could be good for business. What better advertisement for your services than to have accomplished something only a handful of vets in the world have done."

He laughed, which Seb took as a good sign. "I think Federica might object to that. She did almost all of the work."

"You should say that tomorrow. Humility is a good look."

Andrea sank further into himself.

"Come on," Seb rallied. "This is a good thing. You need to take advantage and ride this publicity wave. Maybe into a part-time position at one of the local clinics. They might change their tune about hiring an extra hand when there's a minor celebrity in town."

It took Andrea a long time to reply. "That is what I…" He let out a long, tortured breath. "What Vina and I were fighting about. She wants me to sell the business to Bruno."

"Wait. Whoa. What? To Mr. Punch First, Wallow Drunkenly in the Supply Closet Second?"

"That's what I said!" Andrea finally came to life. "*Si*, he's our cousin. He's family, he needs our help. But that doesn't mean I'm going to sell him our father's legacy! When he has shown no respect, no discipline, no ambition… He pisses on every chance I give him."

"The gay bashing, also not a good look." Seb suddenly wanted to punch something. Or, rather, someone. "You've told her about that, right?"

Andrea vigorously rubbed the back of his neck, which only seemed to further stoke his tension. "It's happened before. He doesn't exactly keep his feelings a secret. From anyone."

"I don't understand. Bruno insults you to the family, loses you clients, hazes you in public, and she thinks you should just surrender your business to that…" Seb held back the word he really wanted to use.

Andrea sighed. "Vina has always felt sorry for him. I mean… I know what he's been through. Fabiana wasn't always the most attentive mother. You saw last night." Seb nodded. "That's why I keep taking him back. He has no one else. But sell him the whole company? *Manco muorto!*"

"Does she think if he has something of his own to take care of, it will make him clean up his act?"

"*Precisamente.*"

"She knows that never works, right?"

Andrea shrugged. "Maybe it does, maybe it doesn't. I just don't understand why it has to be the thing our father worked for his whole life. The thing I've been killing myself over for the past five years. I know they would rather I be a veterinarian. I would rather be one too. But I don't have the money for a clinic, and I would rather do the airport run for the next thirty years than see that *testa di cazzo* run my business into the ground."

Seb caught his hand. Andrea exhaled slowly, trying and failing to vent the buildup of frustration within him.

"Is there a way that you could, I don't know, cut it in half?"

"What do you mean?"

"It's something Henry taught me. Believe it or not, I used to be even more uptight about… well, everything. I'm not really the type of personality that should run their own business, and when I first started bidding for clients and making a name for myself, I had a tendency to overreact. I was miserable at negotiating contract terms. He would always say, 'See if you can cut your demands in half.' Or into thirds, if that doesn't work. Or quarters. Or tenths. Give a little and see what you get back.

"So let's think about Bruno, aka the worst investment imaginable. What does he have that you want? The obvious answer is 'Nothing.' But the real answer is 'Peace.' Or at least peace of mind. That's something you'd be willing to invest in. Minimally. So how do we get you what you want with minimal cost to you? What's his situation? Could he even buy you out, if he wanted to?"

"Not unless he's fucked his way into a bank loan."

"Thanks for that mental image." Seb's full-body shudder earned him a smile. "Vina, kindhearted though she is, hasn't thought her plan through. After all the work you've done, you don't deserve to play debt collector to someone who's already mad at you, with no guarantee that you'll see your investment repaid. But you also need Bruno out of your hair and to keep the women in your family happy. They want to give him a chance to succeed or fail on his terms? Fine. You'll do your part. So the question is, what's the smallest thing you could stand to lose to make them happy and be rid of Bruno for good?"

Andrea had turned his entire body toward him, eyes warm. "You're a prince, you know that?"

"Incorrect. I'm an—"

"Don't say it." He held up a hand, buying some time to think. "If I sold one of my cars at a family discount to Fabiana…"

"That's good. And she owes you."

"But Bruno finds his own clients. No association with me."

"Exactly. Give him just enough rope to hang himself."

But Andrea didn't even crack a smile. "No. Even after everything, I would be happy for his success. For him to finally do some work and stop annoying everyone. *Dio mio*, it would be a blessing. But he doesn't get my father's company. When I sell, if I sell, I sell to someone I know will respect everything my father has done."

Seb squeezed his hand. "See? You cut it in half and found a solution."

"Into fifths, actually. And I'll use the money to buy another car. Or—" A lightning-strike idea suddenly illuminated Andrea's face. "—a van."

"For house-calls? Like a mobile clinic?"

"*Si, si!* If *Zia* Fabi can help Bruno…"

"… she can invest in someone worthwhile for a change. Now you're thinking smart." Seb beamed in approval. "And get a deal on that van, while you're at it, since you're a minor celebrity now."

Andrea smacked him lightly on the cheek, then leaned in to thank him with a kiss.

An odd sense of homecoming overwhelmed Seb as they disembarked, hand in hand. He paused a moment to take in the electric beauty of Amalfi at twilight. The dark surrounding peaks little intimidated the still cobalt-blue sky beyond. Lit archways and porticoes imbued the city's every tier with a lantern glow, from the entrance to the Via Lorenzo d'Amalfi to the converted fort at the far edge of the winding coastal road. Strings of fairy lights decorated the roofs and terraces of most seaside restaurants.

And everywhere, everywhere, the buzz of conversation. People lounged at cafés and strolled along the boardwalk. Jaywalked between the never-ending stream of cars in the Piazza Flavio Gioia. Poured off boats and into tourist buses. Amalfi, the hub of transportation, the most humble of all the coastal towns, the beating heart of the region.

As they meandered off the docks, a chorus of wolf whistles led them to the ladies, perched on the hood of Andrea's SUV while Enzo hid behind the wheel.

"Now don't you two look cozy," Kath coyly remarked before launching herself at them. Seb hadn't been crushed against so many bosoms since his nursing days, but he relished the welcome-home hugs all the same. "How was Capri?"

"Pretty magical." He caught Andrea's eye over the hedge of hair, seeking his confirmation. The smile he received made Seb wish they were alone. But he couldn't resist adding, "Especially the part where I got punched in the stomach."

The cacophony of concern that followed lost him any goodwill with Andrea, who rolled his eyes so far back in their sockets they went zombie white. Seb displayed his bruises with the pride of a war hero; the ladies cooed and hissed on his behalf.

"Don't worry. I kissed it all better," Andrea reassured them as he herded them into the SUV.

"Played doctor, did you?" Maya asked with a pointed wink in Seb's direction.

"Mmm-hmm," Seb confirmed. "You should see his bedside manner."

That earned him a few well-deserved groans. Enzo handed over the keys to Andrea until they discovered there weren't enough seats for everyone. Seb patted his leg suggestively. To his surprise, Andrea gave his brother-in-law the wheel and hopped onto Seb's lap, giving his hips a few extra wriggles to get back at Seb for his double entendres. He shifted to recline against the inner side door so he could hook an arm around Seb's shoulders and face the ladies. Everyone spent most of the short ride giggling about something. Even Enzo cracked a smile at one of Ceri's deadpan pronouncements.

They invaded Marilena's house in high spirits, calling and cooing to their ebullient hostess. As soon as she spotted Seb, she opened her arms to him and crushed him to her chest, whispering another of her Italian enchantments in his ear. Andrea's mother loved to entertain, and she found three enthusiastic guests in the ladies. Once they finished with the introductions, the party spilled onto a small but well-located terrace, the whole of Amalfi spread out beneath. Blue-and-white mosaic tiles dotted with orange flowers mirrored the ceramic plates and bowls on the long wooden table. A curtain of peachy bougainvillea cascaded down from the roof and around the two French doors. A few whimsical statues and overgrown plants added to the homey style. The small apartment revolved around an earth-toned kitchen, where everyone gathered as Enzo played bartender and Marilena put the finishing touches on their feast.

One by one Marilena launched each person off to the table, armed with more booty than a Spanish galleon. Heirloom tomatoes with homemade burrata and basil oil. Smoked mozzarella with lemon leaves and grilled vegetables. Focaccia with caramelized onions and prosciutto. Seafood salad with fat calamari, meaty mussels, and briny clams. A steaming bowl of pasta with zucchini, red peppers, and cream sauce. And for the coup de grace, Enzo and Andrea carried out a gigantic salt-roasted sea bass decorated with slices of lemon the size of Seb's fist.

Marilena waved him over to the place of honor beside her, with Andrea beside him and Vina and Enzo opposite. Chatter reigned over the table as they shared plates and distributed portions. As soon as everyone had what they needed, a hush fell as they gave the incredible meal their due attention. Three resounding "Mmms" from the ladies hit like a conductor's opening taps, and conversation resumed.

Seb learned more about the ladies from Marilena's warm inquiries than he had over multiple nights playing poker with them. Kath and Maya were university roommates who'd lost touch over the years until they ended up working at the same library. Kath's eldest son married one of Maya's foster daughters, so they were both waiting on their first grandchild. Ceri was a marine engineer who'd worked for an oil company optimizing offshore rigs until Hurricane Katrina hit. Now she consulted with the city on levee maintenance and post-BP spill environmental planning. Marilena's voracious curiosity didn't spare Seb, who explained a little bit about his translation work and confirmed that, no, it did not snow year-round in Canada.

When talk turned to sports, specifically Andrea and Enzo's fascination with American football, Seb refocused on his luscious fish. He glanced up to find Marilena's black eyes shining at him. Seb couldn't help but smile back. She squeezed the arm he rested on the table, nudged the white band of skin on his ring finger. Seb hastened to explain, to reassure her he wasn't taken, but Vina cut him off—in perfectly accented French, no less.

"My mother wants to give you her condolences. She heard about your husband."

"Oh!" Seb didn't quite manage to stifle his sigh of relief. "Please give her mine. Andrea told me about your dad."

As Vina translated, Seb glanced over at Andrea, so engrossed by the football talk that he wouldn't have noticed if a bush fire broke out in the bougainvillea.

"She says she is glad to see you going out and enjoying life," Vina continued. "That is the hardest part for her. But of course she is older."

"Doesn't matter how old you are." Seb put a hand over Marilena's. "But she's right. This vacation has helped me more than anything in the past three years."

"She hopes we will see more of you in Amalfi." Vina flickered her gaze to her brother. "I hope so too."

"Well, I'm hoping you guys will let me return some of this amazing hospitality. Have you ever been to Canada?"

Vina's round face blossomed as if she'd turned toward the sun. She hastily related what he'd said to her mother, who crowed with approval.

Laughing, Vina explained, "She would love that."

"Well, I would love to have you." Seb gestured at her pregnant belly. "All of you, when you're ready to travel." He bit the edge of his tongue as he considered whether to make the subtext obvious. "So don't worry about your brother. I'm going to keep in touch."

As soon as he said it, Seb knew it was true. He couldn't make Andrea any promises beyond friendship, but his life would definitely be poorer without him.

Vina scoffed. "If only it were that simple with him."

"He's lucky to have you both to worry so much."

"Ha! He is."

Seb noticed she didn't translate that last bit for her mother. Appeased, Marilena gave his arm a satisfied squeeze. Seb took that as his cue to help with the dishes since his mother raised him right.

Despite their lively hostess' protests, the men cleared the table. Vina, who Seb discovered was a pastry chef who'd studied with French and Belgian masters, snuck in to prepare a sumptuous chocolate almond cake. Enzo quickly shooed her back to the table, reminding her he could slice as well as anyone. Instead she cued up the stereo with some Sinatra-era classics, which raised a cheer from the balcony. By the time Seb brought out the dessert plates, Marilena had broken out the limoncello, and the ladies dragged her onto the impromptu dance floor.

Seb tried to hide, crouching in the far corner behind Enzo as he scarfed down his cake. But when Kath did her best Patrick Swayze in his direction, he downed a shot of limoncello and gave over to the music. Fortunately the ladies only needed a sturdy body to swing them around—and swing from him they did, passing him back and forth like a bottle of cheap wine. He barely had time to simper over Andrea dancing with his mom before Ceri swooped away, and Maya and Kath took her place.

"Ooh, a threesome." Seb tucked each lady under an arm for a weird bit of halfhearted Greek dancing. "Insert obvious kink joke here."

"Counters with crack about impressing your future in-laws." Maya cackled, pleased with herself. Seb gave her the stink-eye. "Too soon?"

"No comment."

The ladies shared a look.

"Gossip update." Kath tried to play it cool but looked fit to burst with it. "Ceri is ditching us and extending her stay."

"What?! For Lucia?"

"She wants to see where it goes," Maya said, skeptical. "And there's only one way to do that."

"After two days? That's…"

"Do I need to say it?"

Seb snorted. "No."

"I will." Kath sighed. "Lesbians. I swear, it's been this way her whole life. She once parlayed flirting at a truck stop into a five-year relationship."

"When you know, you know," Seb quipped, mostly to deflect the heat off of him. He hadn't been feeling any pressure until that very moment, even with all the 'meet the family' chaos. But hearing everyone else's expectations for him and Andrea got him twitching.

Because he wasn't ready for anything serious. Or any long-distance relationships, for that matter. Henry may have been dead three years, but Seb had only taken his first real breath since losing him in the past week. He was getting his groove back, not plunging into another decade or more of commitment.

"So this one." Kath interrupted his thoughts.

"Oh, you just have to go there," Maya grumbled.

"Are you ashamed?"

"Not for a second. But don't act out because you're jealous."

"Will someone please tell me what's going on?" Seb begged.

"Gerardo and Maya, sitting in a—Well, more like knocking boots till dawn." Kath giggled. "I was next door. Didn't get a lick of sleep."

"You had your chance when he said he loved strawberries."

"Uh, I think she's saving her freebie five for someone way better than him," Seb remarked.

"Boom!" Kath gave him a high-five.

"So," he turned to Maya, "what position does swarthy Gerardo play?"

She put her hand over her mouth to contain her laugher. "Striker. But he misses the goal at least half the time."

"Ugh." Seb shook his head so that mental image didn't get stuck. "Dodged a bullet there, Kathy."

"Wish I'd been quick enough to avoid it," Maya concluded. "Damn limoncello."

"Oh, I don't know." Seb watched as Andrea passed his mom over to Enzo, then sauntered over to the stereo. After a quick search of her playlists, the music switched from up-tempo big band to the sultry slink of Nina Simone. "Wild is the Wind," one of Seb's all-time favorites. His heartbeat sped up as Andrea moved toward him. "It's worked out pretty well for me thus far."

Later he wouldn't remember how the ladies disappeared, how everyone and everything around them misted into an impressionistic blur, how they came together. They started in the standard dance position as the last shimmers of sunlight hazed the edges of the horizon. A dark velvet blue cloaked the city, pinprick stars and fulsome flames their only illumination. Burnished as a bronze statue in the candlelight, Andrea's hard-cut features echoed the faces of ancient statesmen—patrician, with a few florid accents. Such as his lips, which he brushed teasingly over Seb's before he rested his head in the crook of his neck. Seb hugged him in so they swayed more than danced, giving over to the moment, to the moonlight, to the man who summoned him back from the underworld with the warmth and sweetness of Ceres.

When his conscious mind woke a couple of hours later, Seb reclined against a mossy stone wall in a shadowy garden. The lights of Amalfi peeked through the slits in the cliffside gate. Andrea lay spread out beside him, Seb's thigh pillowing his head and his fingers tangled in the black waves of his hair. They had slipped out of the party sometime earlier, ostensibly so Andrea could show Seb the lemon grove. He doubted that excuse fooled anyone but the willfully ignorant, especially given how they couldn't seem to peel away from each other after their dance, errant limbs drawn back as if by magnetic force. Seb had pretended to be enchanted by the garden until they passed beyond shouting distance. Then Andrea started sucking on his neck, and Seb curved his hands around his taut ass, and they let themselves be engulfed by the fire that ever simmered between them.

Seb petted Andrea's heavy head, wondering if the past two days of no sleep had finally caught up with him. He should have known better.

"So my mother tells me we are planning a trip to Canada?"

Seb let out a rueful groan. "Sorry. I didn't know what to say. She wants so much for you. For us."

"No, I think you were right the first time." He shifted onto his back, stared up into the ceiling of interwoven branches. "I'm not sure my mamma and me have the same picture of my future in mind."

"I don't think any parent really understands what their adult child wants. They cling to things that symbolize stability, security, but… life isn't always like that."

Andrea grinned up at him. "More Henry wisdom?"

"I did teach him a few things, you know." Seb bristled.

"I am certain you did." Andrea ran a finger along the soft skin behind Seb's knee, making him shiver.

"And you are welcome. I mean… I hope it's not overstepping to invite you to come visit me. If you want to."

"Overstepping?"

"This little arrangement of ours."

"Ah." Andrea took some time digesting this, his expressive eyes reflecting only the shade of the leaf cover.

More time than Seb would have liked. He sat there, pleading into the night, that nothing would change. That they would continue as they were till next Sunday, till Seb went home and got some perspective on his whirlwind holiday. Because he knew he was swept up in the sea and the sky, in the spell of Amalfi and Andrea, and this was all a temporary reality. A fever dream of a life that would eventually burn out, or burn him. And he had suffered enough.

"And it doesn't have to be…" Seb couldn't suppress the sudden urge to fill the air with words. All the words. A suit of armor's worth of words. "*We* don't have to be like we are now. I mean, if we're there, and single, and we want to… Then that would be fun too. But I meant it when I said your family's invited. I just don't want to lose touch with you after this. Everything has been amazing—beyond amazing—the past week, and I'm really looking forward to the next few days. But if, when you come to Canada, you're in a different place, then… I still want to see you. I would like it if we could be friends. I mean, we are friends. I feel like you're a friend. You've helped me so much, and I—"

Andrea, now crouched in front of him, pressed a finger to his lips.

"*Piano, piano*, Sebastiano." Andrea kissed him on the forehead, stroked through his long, loose hair. "Let us not make promises we might not be able to keep."

He rose, straightened his rumpled clothes. Seb took a moment to yank back the reins on his racing emotions. Just what had he been about to say? With a shaking hand, he gripped Andrea's offered arm and staggered to his feet.

"We should get back," he suggested with a lightness he didn't feel. "God knows what they've gotten up to."

To no one's surprise, as soon as the boys had disappeared, the cards came out. Marilena and her widows' circle met for poker and gossip every Friday night, and she had the bags of seashells to prove it. By the time he and Andrea returned, they were thick as thieves, sipping limoncello and critiquing each other's stakes in two languages. Vina and Enzo had texted their goodbyes to Andrea before rushing off to catch their friend's boat back to Capri. Not wanting to interrupt his mother's fun, Seb and Andrea instead cleared the last of the plates, grabbed themselves a pair of frilly aprons, and stuck into dish duty.

Chapter Twelve

THE SOUND OF MIDNIGHT
ECHOES THROUGH THE SATED HEARTS
OF NEWFOUND LOVERS
-#107, *In Blue Solitudes*, S. Wilson-Osaki

Seb stood on the upper deck of the Villa Napolitana in the dead of night, listening. The choir of chirping crickets almost drowned out the fainter sounds: the flap of hanging laundry in the faint breeze, the honk of a distant horn, the hum of an air conditioner in one of the lower apartments. He inhaled deep of the sunburned smell of the city. His eyes scanned the panoramic view, from the pockmarked face of the mountainside to the peak-a-boo glimpse of the sea between two aged buildings to the anemone-like fountain in the villa's courtyard. Seb wanted to engrave every detail of this enchanted place into his mind in case he never saw it again.

His last night in Amalfi. Sleepless like so many others, but not for the same reasons. Something stirred in him he couldn't put a name to—he suspected it was the thrill of being alive after grieving for so long. It nagged him out of bed, and Andrea's arms, to commune with the night. It lured him out of doors clad in only his sarong. Made him restless, impatient. Gave him midnight daydreams. Convinced him he missed a place he hadn't even left yet.

With a final tip of his invisible hat to the moon, Seb crept back into the apartment and up to the loft. His sleeping beauty hadn't stirred. Still curled around the pillow Seb had slipped in to replace himself, Andrea in slumber murmured to an imaginary menagerie, forever soothing injured beasts. After easing open one of the shutters so he could forgo the lamp, Seb snuck into the bedside armchair and cracked open his journal. He'd kept a makeshift diary over the past few days, jotting down memories and anecdotes he would later spin into verse. He felt too close to his holiday adventures to do more than scrawl down a few initial impressions. Time and distance would fog them over enough to blur the details.

After catching the boat back from Maiori, he and the ladies had toasted their last round of poolside G&Ts. Andrea swung by just in time to watch himself on the evening news, updating everyone on the health of Federica and her twin foals. Seb could practically hear the women of Amalfi's collective swoon echo through the valley. Not that seeing Andrea look so poised and professional had a different effect on him. If anything he stood taller as he later escorted Andrea down the main street. Every shopkeeper and cab driver stopped to shout their compliments. The waiters at Marina Grande—where Seb treated Andrea to dinner— even sung some Italian ditty as they waltzed in. They took the long way back, strolling through the backstreets hand in hand, their enjoyment of each other's company a potent brand of foreplay.

Seb left his pen hanging as the night's passion played out for him again. Andrea's sinuous frame strung tight as a violin's bow. Seb, in total command of his instrument, plucked at each of his concerns and trepidations, strummed him into submission with a practiced hand, wrung from him the sweetest moaning music. He'd blanketed Andrea with his body until sleep finally seized him, praying an impression of him molded itself into Seb's skin. Reminded himself in a weak moment he would see him tomorrow evening, in Sorrento. That only his love affair with Amalfi was coming to an end.

A finger of milky sunlight clung to the bottom of the page. Just as Seb looked to the window, Andrea's alarm blared. A muffled groan heralded the zombie lurch of a hand out from under the covers. Andrea smashed a fist down on the digital clock, flopped it onto the night table like a dying fish. The flashing-red time: 4:45 a.m.

Andrea groaned, then, with a mouthful of pillow, "Sebastiano?"

"*Sì.*" Seb set his journal aside, dropped his sarong, and eased back into bed. With greedy arms, Andrea pulled him back into his cocoon of warmth. "What time is your first pickup?"

"Too soon." He shifted Seb on top of him, perhaps as a shield against the encroaching day. "You smell like the ocean."

"I went outside for a bit."

"For a swim?"

"Dipped my feet in the pool."

"Mmm." Andrea's body relaxed so much Seb feared he'd fallen back to sleep. "Is it cold now, in Canada?"

"Not really. But the leaves will have started to change."

"They will burn the fields here soon. You can already see the smoke when you drive over the mountain."

"That always seemed strange to me. Scorching everything."

"So it can grow again next year." His gray-green eyes reflected only Seb in the filmy dawn light. "Will you come back?"

"I'm not gone yet."

Andrea cupped his face to hold it aloft, fixed his enigmatic gaze on him. "Will you?"

Seb swallowed hard. "I want to. I hope so. But it's like you said…"

"No promises." Andrea sighed, closed his eyes. "*Si.*"

His Adam's apple bobbed once, twice; he exhaled a shaky breath. He found Seb's lips by memory, his kisses merciless in their ardor. Andrea gripped into his back until his nails scraped bloody half-moons into his skin. Seb would later notice them in the bathroom mirror, alien footprints on the banks of the Sea of Tranquility.

A few rough gyrations, and Seb felt the stab of Andrea's cockhead into the still-tender bruises on his abdomen. He reached down to tug him to full stiffness, swallowed a whine as Andrea tongue fucked his mouth. Swinging them round so their jabbing hips locked into alignment, he yanked Andrea's head back by the hair as they found their rhythm: whip fast, pounding, crazy beautiful.

Andrea clamped his lids shut, squinting, as if to mark

every second, every touch, every sizzle of sensation. Andrea smoothed a hand across Seb's face, reading him, memorizing. Seb loosed his grip on everything save their grinding pricks. Eyes wide, he watched Andrea thrash and gasp as if witnessing a miracle. Which, in a way, it was—the resurrection of Seb's heart. When his hips began to stutter, Seb gave them a slap, spurring him on.

Wanting more. Wanting everything.

A cry ripped out of him, gut deep and wild. Seb welcomed the hot splash on his stomach, the torrents of pleasure. Andrea pinned him to the mattress as he howled his last, then crashed, dead weight, on top of him. A flutter of lashes against his neck, a savage bite into the base of his throat.

In Italian, a whispered farewell. Seb claimed a last, sensuous kiss, gave in to sleep's dark undertow.

Seb should have recognized it for the goodbye it was.

He sat on the top step of his nemesis, the staircase at the Villa Napolitana, as he had for the past two hours, watching the sun crawl across the sky. His suitcase stretched out nearby, soaking in the rays, noncommittal. His phone hung limp in one of the lower pockets of his cargo shorts. He'd sealed it in an hour ago, exasperated with catching the sun's glare on the screen and thinking he'd gotten a text. Or a call. Or any form of communication from Andrea, who never showed up to drive him to Sorrento.

Seb slumped against the stucco wall that lined the apartment-level deck. He knew he should leave, should move on, should shrug Andrea off like a too-heavy layer of clothing. Andrea had cast him off that easily. But his absence crushed into his chest, a pile of rocks to which each passing minute added more weight. Seb kept flashing back to that night three years ago, moved through the same stages of impatience, annoyance, anger, concern to… where? Fear? There would be no telltale knock at the door this time. There was one rational explanation that let Andrea off the hook for ditching him, but his brain couldn't bring itself to go there. Even Seb's karma wasn't that bad.

Was it?

He suppressed the urge to send a third text. In truth, he didn't have the energy. He stared down the endless flight of stairs, considered pitching forward.

A hand fell on his shoulder. Kath's ruddy cheeks shined in defiance of her melancholy eyes. "Hon, we have to get going if we're going to catch the ferry."

"Mmm."

"We've called a porter to help us down with our bags."

"Mmm."

She looked over his head at Maya. Seb could imagine the looks they exchanged but didn't care. He would never see Andrea again. Just like he would never see Henry again.

His heart shivered like a frightened rabbit. His throat spasmed; his hands shook. Heat leeched out of him until he felt brittle and hollow as a husk. The light hurt, sights and sounds bullying his senses into a corner. His father was gone.

Henry was gone. Andrea was gone. Everyone left him, everyone left him, everyone left him...

Seb doubled over, head between his knees. He wheezed in breath after breath, buttressed his hands against something solid: wood and stone. He started the count back from one hundred, concentrated on visualizing the numbers. Focused as many senses as possible on a mundane task. Automatic as opposed to instinctual, overriding his panic. What would his therapist say? Climb back down the ladder rung by rung. Don't look down.

When he felt ready, he lifted his head. Kath crouched in front of him, holding a glass of water. Maya had replaced her at his side. He murmured his thanks, downed the glass in one go. Measured out several cleansing breaths.

"Is it okay if I come with you?"

"Of course, cher." Maya pet a hand over his head. "Do you want us to stay an extra day? Gerardo has a contact in Sorrento—"

"No. It's enough that we're going there together." Seb straightened, got his bearings. "Sorry. It's kind of a sore point, people leaving and never coming back." His voice broke on the last word, but he soldiered through.

The ladies nodded, hugged him but didn't press. Seb let the business of their departure overtake him: the final check of his apartment, the arrival of the porter, the packing of the golf cart that would take them down to the docks, their final moments in the Villa Napolitana. When he woken that morning, he was so certain he would return one day. Now... well.

The ride down Amalfi's main street passed too quickly.

No sooner had he caught his last glimpse of the duomo than they zoomed through the final archway, out to the marina. In the rush to buy tickets and the race for the ferry, Seb didn't have time to linger over any ambivalent or mournful emotions. As the boat sped away, Amalfi had already begun to disappear in his mind, a series of impressions and—he had to admit—triumphs that would forever be cast in a somber hue.

Seb parked at the back of the boat, staring out at Amalfi until they rounded the cape at Praiano. As he ambled through the aisles to rejoin the ladies, Seb struggled to quell the emotion rising within him, to conclude the too-brief chapter of his stay in paradise. What kind of author was he if he couldn't write the final lines? Had Seb been so focused on his own character arc that he failed to flesh out Andrea's? Or maybe that's what Andrea objected to all along, having a narrative imposed on him. His last act as Seb's lover was one of self-determination. A *cri de coeur.*

Or maybe he just didn't want to deal with Seb's bullshit anymore.

The clink of glasses guided him toward a bench in the back. Happy hour for the ladies spanned from noon till bedtime, so Seb grabbed his cocktail and nestled between them. He forced as much good cheer as he could muster into a toast since he was glad he had met them and would cherish their friendship. And if a hint of sadness tinged their kind faces when they smiled, he felt only gratitude. At being understood. For their welcome and their encouragement. For finding a pair of surrogate mothers while searching for himself.

"So… to New Year's in N'Orleans?" Kath raised her glass.

"Am I invited?" Seb asked.

Maya chuckled. "Of course you are, cher. We'll find you a hot Cajun who needs to practice his English."

"Operation *Acadiens*?"

"*Ouaille*."

"Sounds…" Seb huffed a breath, unable to rouse to the occasion. "I'll definitely be there."

Kath cradled his free arm. "You know the real tragedy in all this would be if you stopped travelling. You get that, right?"

"Please tell me this isn't a 'keep it in your pants' lecture."

"N-no." Kath considered her next words. "It's a 'keep it in your pants if you can't handle the fallout' lecture."

Seb grumbled. "Point taken."

"Well, I, for one, don't think it's a fair one." Maya craned her body around to address Kath directly. "None of us expected Andrea to react the way he has. To promise one thing and then run away like a…"

"Coward," Seb supplied.

"Exactly." Maya grunted, bullish. "Be a man. If there's a conversation to be had, have it. Don't just shirk your professional responsibilities. Wasn't that his entire point with Bruno?"

Seb smacked his lips, a bitter taste curdling his mouth. "It was."

"And did you?" Kath inquired. "Did the two of you discuss… possibilities?"

That brought Seb up short. "Possibilities like what?"

"I don't know… Trying out a long-distance relationship, staying in Amalfi a couple more weeks, getting together in six months to see if the flame's still there…"

"I invited him to Canada," Seb admitted. "As a friend, more or less. I said that if he came, we could see where we are… But that I definitely wanted to keep in touch. I didn't want to lose him."

Both ladies opened their mouths to speak but ended up shaking their heads.

"Oh, cher." Maya tapped the hand holding his glass, urging him to drink. "And he still didn't show up? That's…"

"We've been reading this wrong." Kath sighed. "Wrong, wrong, wrong."

A furrow marred Seb's brow. "Explain."

"We thought you'd taken Operation Stella a bit too literally," Maya said.

"I mean, we all know how the real thing turned out," Kath added. "Not to mention holiday romances in general."

"And watching the two of you on Sunday… Cher, Andrea was smitten. We could see you not seeing the stars in his eyes."

"We were afraid for him, weren't we, M? You even said, 'That boy is gonna get his heart broke before this is all over.'"

"And he's a sweep. A giver. We never thought he'd ask for what he wanted, which so clearly was you."

"Stop." Seb shut his eyes. Wished he could block his ears as well, but he wasn't, you know, five. "So what? You think he didn't show not because he didn't want me, but because he wanted me too much?"

"That's just the thing," Kath said. "We thought he stayed away because he couldn't bring himself to say goodbye. But if you'd already given him hope there could be more…"

Maya growled, mostly to herself. "The boy's just greedy. And unrealistic. What does he expect, for you to rearrange your life on a whim? You've just emerged from your grief, you've only known him for a little over a week—"

"He's a Matt, though," Kath interjected.

"A Michael, cher." At her confusion, Maya elaborated: "Queer references, not straight ones."

"I personally think of myself as more of a Miranda," Seb quipped, to the ladies' delight. "At least now that Henry is gone. And you, my dear, with your Gerardo-shagging ways, are a proud Samantha. And you…" He playfully considered Kath. "Would you be insulted if I said Charlotte?"

"Gosh, no. So long as I'm not a Carrie, any of the others is good."

"I couldn't agree more." Seb pecked them on the cheek. "Now that we've covered all the pop culture bases, do you think I could continue drowning my sorrows?"

"Only if you promise not to let this get you down for good." Maya slouched down again so he could rest his head on her shoulder. "Remember, the point of Stella getting her groove back wasn't that she found herself a man. It was that she found herself."

"Amen to that," Kath concurred, raising her glass for a final toast.

"Do you think I should have discussed it more openly with him? Do you think I should have offered him more?"

"Good morning to you too," Maya deadpanned from her hotel room in Assisi.

Through the phone, but Seb could tell by the tone of her voice. She didn't sound groggy, so he hadn't woken her up. Probably. He'd waited till nearly ten to call, five hours after he snapped awake in his Sorrento hotel room, pert as the mechanical, lederhosen-clad figures in a cuckoo clock. That someone forgot to wind. His movements as sluggish as his pulse, Seb hadn't quite managed to drag himself out of bed. Or stop thinking.

"Should I have made it clearer how I was feeling? How I'm not ready for… I don't know." He stared up at the stucco ceiling as if a pattern could be deciphered from its swipes and squiggles. "I feel like I've just learned to breathe again."

"Do you want me to put him on speakerphone?" A cranky background mutter from Kath put an end to that notion. "All right. I've got fifteen minutes, cher."

"Sorry. I should… I'll let you go."

"Under no circumstances." She sipped something, which made him think of coffee. He should have called room service first. "Why the retread? Has Andrea contacted you?"

"No." Seb exhaled a long, shaky breath. "I just wanted to make sure that I haven't been unfair to him somehow."

"Andrea is a grown-ass man. If he wanted something more with you or didn't like the way you were treating him, he should have said something about it. He did the opposite of that."

"I know…"

A pause. He could hear Maya and Kath trading looks over the silence.

"Where is this coming from?"

Seb had an answer, he really did. He hadn't just lain there, alternating between ache, befuddlement, and fury, for five hours. At least not the full five hours.

"I got used to it again. Waking up to someone. Knowing that they're there through the night."

"Oh, cher."

"I can't tell if this is actually about Andrea or just me wanting that again. Or missing it… I don't know." He starfished his legs and arms out to shoo away any ghosts haunting his space. "Am I clinging to this idea of him because I really felt something for him, or because he was around when I was feeling vulnerable?"

"Only you can answer that." Another sip. "Andrea seems to have made his feelings clear."

Seb swallowed hard, nodded into the receiver. "He did."

"It's important to think these things through, don't get me wrong. And I know you feel… robbed of something. But would you feel that way if you'd gotten your goodbye? Would you be questioning it if things had gone your way?"

The Rorschach-test ceiling mocked him with its impenetrability, same as his own wants, needs, desires.

"Point."

"You need to stop chasing down the ones who are already gone, cher, and find someone who'll stick around."

"Game, set, and match."

"I thought we used soccer metaphors. Don't confuse me. I'm geeky, not sporty."

"You're stellar. Not to mention an angel for putting up with me." Seb wished he could hug her. "Go have an amazing day. You're officially disinvited from my pity party."

"You go out and have some fun, Agent Seb." Her drill sergeant's voice didn't have enough bark to make him piddle himself, but he still shook in his boots. "Operation Stella is done. Welcome to Operation Shirley Valentine."

"Uh, I think I missed that one?"

"Rent it. When you get home. Because from now on, you'll be too busy to sulk in your hotel room."

Despite himself, Seb felt a smile creep across his face. "Thanks, Maya. Meeting you has made this trip worth it."

"Stop trying to butter me up and go get yourself an espresso. You're going to have a busy day."

Chapter Thirteen

> HIS EARS BEND AROUND
> THE EDGES OF THE DOOR, BUT
> THE KNOCK NEVER COMES
> -#88, *IN BLUE SOLITUDES*, S. WILSON-OSAKI

Sun baked and swoon giddy, Seb climbed the ancient stone steps to Pompeii's Villa of the Mysteries, slow as a pilgrim seeking enlightenment. After getting turned around more than once in the courtyard maze of knee-high shrubs—but somehow never making it under the column-supported roof—a slinky white cat stalked across his path. A flick of her tail, and Seb followed her into the fresco-lined corridors, their blood reds and opulent golds eroded by volcanic ash.

Something wasn't right. Though dust motes spiraled in the beams of sunlight that shined through the cracks in the ceiling, Seb shivered, a mordant damp biting into his bones. The stench of bilious gas and brimstone soot clogged his lungs, making him cough. As he lurched on, half-heard rustles and skitters had him glancing over his shoulder.

His feline guide—who bore a striking resemblance to Nagiko—led him into a remote, shadowy room. From nowhere a torch fired to life, found its way into his hand. Here the frescoes had been preserved in breathtaking detail: a copper-haired beauty flanked by two cupids, a heartbroken man with his head burrowed in his mother's lap, a winged figure with spear raised, a devious boy holding up a terrifying mask. The more Seb observed, the more vividly the scene played out before his eyes, a Dionysian rite that somehow held the answer to all his questions.

It started with a flick of a hand. Then the flap of a toga. A dancing figure began to twist and twirl. Seb could discern the tinkle of jewels, the crinkle of a scroll, the strum of a lyre. The vibrant scene burst into life, its players singing and chanting, sobbing and bleating with Seb in the role of stunned audience. He staggered back into the suddenly dark corridor, feeling the air with outstretched hands until his little white guardian curled her tail around his ankle.

Seb caught her up in his arms, burying his face in her downy fur. Her purrs reverberated against his cheek; he found his center. Forcing his breaths to slow, his pulse to temper, he looked up to discover himself in the villa's central hall. A long rectangular room built around a middle skylight framed by columns that acted as a sort of moon dial. Through the gap in the ceiling, towering Vesuvius loomed against an angry sky. Flashes of lightning illuminated a ring of doomsday storm clouds around the volcano's peak.

A sonic boom electrified the air. Steam shot out of the crater, which vomited hot spews of lava over its edge and down its slopes. The cat clawed into Seb's arm, sped off. He stood paralyzed, disbelieving. This couldn't be happening again. Not now. Not to him. Not after…

"It's begun," a too-familiar voice beside him whispered, awestruck.

Seb wrenched away from the scene of imminent destruction but somehow wasn't surprised to see Henry there. Face beaming with wonderment and glee as it always did when facing down impossible odds—like convincing Seb to marry him when he was only twenty-three.

"What has?" Seb asked, because what else could he do with a ghost?

"The inevitable." Henry turned, regarded him with a look so intimate Seb had to fight against his welling tears. If these were their last moments together, he wanted to witness every second. He pushed into his arms until Henry cupped his face with silky hands—hands too soft to be those of a lifelong traveler, or so Seb always teased him. Henry's giving stare bore into him, beheld him as no one else ever would. "Be brave."

Seb drew him in for a kiss. The kiss he tried to give Henry's cold, broken body on the slab in the coroner's office, his blood caked on the sheet that covered the worst of it. The last time he ever held him was in death.

But here he was: warm, thrumming, alive. The scrape of his stubble and the soft of his lips, here, at the end of the world. The Villa of the Mysteries had conjured her final marvel, and Seb hugged him hard, drinking in Henry's rich, clean scent. The scent of pine and smoke and twenty-five-year-old scotch. The feel of a loose flannel shirt and worn denim. Of wiry, bedraggled, bon mot-ed Henry—his husband. The only man he'd ever loved.

The feeling of wrongness crept over him again, spiders

scuttling over his skin, but Seb only clung to Henry. Thunder crashed and the sky erupted. The ground quaked. The ceiling crumbled. The wind battered them into a corner. A shower of ash had them cowering.

"Be brave!" Henry shouted into the storm, then screamed...

... shrill as a referee's whistle, straight into his ear. Seb jolted awake. Head spinning, vision swimming with images from his dream, he grabbed hold of the armrests as the train squealed to a stop. Panting and sweating as if he'd just sprinted a mile, Seb focused on the seat in front of him, some sort of coat of arms stamped into the leather.

When finally he felt stable enough to look outside, the rush of relief that he had not missed his station was replaced by one of dread. Of going back to that luxe but sterile hotel room. Of another night wandering the piazzas of Sorrento, praying for his phone to chime. Of the empty chair at the other end of his dining table, stealing away his appetite.

After downing the last of his water, he searched his backpack for the stack of restaurant cards Andrea had given him on that first ride from the airport.

Seb knew what he had to do.

***

The shadow of Monte Solaro crept across the sea toward the Faraglioni, seeking to blight out their golden-hour luster. Seb lounged on a tiled bench under the palm trees of the

Giardini di Augusto, slurping down a *granita al limone* from the stand just outside the gates. He'd come to watch the sun set, not accounting for the south-facing location of the garden and the mountain to its west. As metaphors went, it was appropriate. His second afternoon in Capri had been plagued by deep thoughts: of Henry, of Andrea, of his place in the world, of his ambitions for his post-vacation life. Of equal parts excitement and melancholy for this, his last night in Italy.

No question as to where he would spend it. When finally the encroaching twilight extinguished the gilt peaks of the Faraglioni, Seb bid the crocodile's teeth a fond farewell and strolled up the Via Vittorio Emanuele toward the Piazzetta, the central square. He, and likely other tourists, used its storybook clock tower as something of a compass needle, orienting them toward the different points of interest in Capri Town. A twitch of nerves seized his shoulders as he veered down the Via Roma toward the dainty pink building that housed the best restaurant on the island, Fabiana's.

After checking his hair in a storefront window, Seb straightened his suit and his posture before shoving his way down the crammed sidewalk. He'd hemmed and hawed for most of the morning over making reservations but decided to just pop in. It felt rebellious to leave something so important to chance. His fairy godmother had bibbidy-bobbidy-booed him into the arms of two princes thus far. Hopefully her wand had a few drops of magic left to enchant this evening.

A few steps from the door, Seb almost lost his nerve. He considered ducking into the far more traditional trattoria across the way, with its gingham tablecloths and its garish ceramic dishes, to people watch until the next ferry. But the silken voice of a 1930s torch singer lured him closer. Passing the alley that led to the lower-level kitchen door, a fragrance so savory and sensuous as to tempt a nun wafted up, tantalizing his senses. The memory of her gnocchi, little potato clouds in a decadent sauce, erased any further doubts. Come what may on the romantic score, Seb deserved this final feast.

"My little savior!" exclaimed the savviest hostess on the island just as Seb gave up hope of securing a table. "Oh, how wonderful to see you back here, Sébastien."

The stiff-lipped maître d', among the missing staff last weekend, had attempted to swat him away once Seb admitted to not having a reservation. A few discreet words in Italian from Fabiana, and suddenly a seat opened up in the bar section. The lady herself escorted him down once Seb offered her his arm, petting his hand and complimenting the very same suit he'd worn a week ago as if she'd never set eyes on it.

"I hear I missed quite a party last Sunday. Lena had so much fun with your lady friends she almost slept through our weekly trip to the farmers' market."

"They were singing her praises too. I'd wager you'll see them back here next summer." Seb kept an eye on the waiters swinging in and out of the kitchen doors, trying to send the message that he looked for a certain someone.

"You must tell them they have a standing invitation if they do come back."

"They'll be thrilled to hear it." He leaned in conspiratorially. "They were pretty jealous when I told them how I spent last Saturday night."

"Forgetting to mention you were on your feet for most of it?"

"Possibly…"

Her laugh, like the trill of a songbird, drew more than a few predatory eyes in their direction. No wonder Chef Mauro hid in the kitchen, where he could put his knives to better use. Fabiana received this attention as if it was her birthright, nodding and waving to her subjects. Though she steered Seb to a quiet corner table by the floor-to-ceiling windows—with an unimpeded view of the staircase, he noticed—he felt as if he were the consort and she the queen. He wondered how drunk he would have to get her before he unlocked her treasure trove of gossip and secrets.

"Order anything you want, bello. I insist." She squeezed his shoulders as he perused the specials. "It's my pleasure to treat you. After all, you're practically family."

She floated away, hopefully to her office to call a certain fair-weather lover Seb missed something fierce.

He people watched through his first two courses, too wound up to manage anything more than a few scribbles in his journal. Seb switched to one of the romances Kath had passed along to him—a fantastic historical about a monk who falls for a Viking during the Dark Ages—but he glanced up every time someone clopped down the stairs or swept through the kitchen door. Given the waiters came and went once every .3 seconds, he'd absorbed approximately two and a half paragraphs in over an hour. Just when Seb decided to solve *for* x and pull out his phone, he felt a presence at his side.

He forced out the breath he'd been holding for the past four days. All the arguments and apologies he'd reasoned out escaped him now that the moment had come, but Seb didn't care. He would listen first—he'd made that silent promise to Andrea in absentia, and to himself. So long as no one sucker punched him—again—they would work it out.

Seb glanced up to find Bruno looming over him and almost passed out. It took every ounce of his self-control not to shrink away. Both his stomach and left cheek braced for a blow, though he didn't think even Bruno was stupid enough to assault him twice and believe he'd get away with it. Seb stared up at him with as much menace as he could muster—which, truth be told, was probably not a lot—until he noticed the younger man trembled.

"*Signor* Osakay." The mistake was far less charming in Bruno's mumble mouth. "I talk to you, please."

"About what?"

Bruno worked his jaw, whether out of resentment or lack of vocabulary, Seb couldn't tell. He sighed, then gestured for him to sit, if only to spare the inevitable crick in his neck from looking up at him. After a long moment's hesitation, Bruno dropped into the opposite chair. Now that Bruno wasn't snarling in his face, Seb could appreciate how Andrea hadn't gotten all the looks in the family. Seb wouldn't drop trou for the broody Italian surfer vibe Bruno had going on, but plenty of women would. Bruno's tragic history with the ladies really was down to his attitude, a fact multiple family members must have mentioned to him. But then listening hadn't ever been the guy's strong suit, in said family members' opinions.

"My English is no good. But I want to say sorry. For…" Seb's abs tensed as Bruno mimicked the stomach punch he'd dealt him the week before. "*Molto, molto* sorry. I was… *rabbioso…* with my…"

"Andrea."

"*Si, mio cugino.* He is *molto severo,* for long time. Give me many problems."

"And I suppose you never did anything to deserve them."

Bruno shrugged in classic Italian style, nowhere near matching the panache of his cousin.

Seb was already done with this apology. "He didn't hit me. You did. And threatened us all at the *calcio* match. I don't care how many '*moltos*' you add. 'Sorry' isn't good enough."

Bruno nodded vigorously but grit his teeth, still the lion in the lamb suit.

"Vina, she tell me you *persuadere* Andrea to… sell auto to me."

That made Seb straighten in his seat. "He took my advice, you mean?"

"Si. Vina say. So I sorry. I don't like you are *ricchione*, but you are good *ricchione*."

"Do I want to know what that means?"

"You know…" He performed a crude gesture Seb didn't particularly want to interpret.

"Right." The last drop of Seb's patience evaporated in the heat of his anger. No amount of responsibility was going to make a silk purse out of this sow's ear, and his family had been learning that the hard way. He almost regretted his advice to Andrea, but at least Bruno would be out of his hair for a while. "I care nothing about what you think of me or my life, considering how much you tend to get violently drunk and assault strangers. But in the spirit of my late husband, here's some advice: You've been given another chance. Don't fuck it up."

To his surprise, Bruno laughed. "You also smart *ricchione*. I do like you say."

Seb countered with a shrug. "Time will tell."

Bruno smacked the table; Seb shuddered. The brute raised two pacifying hands, muttering further apologies in Italian. Seb suspected if he looked up "bull in a china shop" in the dictionary, he'd find Bruno's picture. If the guy had a kinder disposition, it might be almost cute; instead his clumsiness only worsened his adult temper tantrums.

Seb forced a smile on his face, desperate for him to leave. Bruno stood, lumbered over to Seb's side, again emphasizing the difference in their positions. Seb leaned away, avoiding the hand Bruno sought to place on his shoulder. When Bruno instead proffered that hand for him to shake, Seb desperately wanted to protest, refuse, anything. His obliviousness to Seb's discomfort was another strike against him. No wonder Bruno's ex-girlfriend leapt at the chance to bed Andrea after suffering this oaf.

Seb stared at his hand much longer than necessary but saw no other option. He gave it a quick shake.

"*Bene.*" At least one of them was satisfied. "I see you in Amalfi, *Signor* Osakay."

Seb couldn't think of anything he wanted to be less true.

"Not if I see you first," he muttered, signaling to his

waiter for a refill on the wine.

By the time the witching hour struck, Seb pushed the crumbs of his second slice of torta caprese around his plate with the tines of his fork. He occasionally glanced at the stairs but found more solace in the black void of the view. The glass reflected the bright goings-on behind him like an early film screen, a busy shadow play of motion and oversized gestures set to a jazzy soundtrack. Fabiana's swung with the verve of a Gatsby party while Seb sat at the edge of the dock, pining for the green light across the lake. But was Henry or Andrea his Daisy? Seb always thought Gatsby should give up the ladies and shack up with Nick, anyway.

With the toll of a distant bell, the countdown had begun. One hour till the hydrofoil he had arranged to bring him back to the mainland cast off, ten until he had to leave for the airport, twelve before his flight to Rome, fifteen before he took off back to a drizzly late September in Montreal. Seb burrowed into his armchair, the acid burn of this second rejection souring his stomach and spinning his head. He had honestly thought Andrea would come. Though he couldn't be certain whether the roulette wheel of fate had spun in his favor with so many variables—Red or black? Red or black? Come on, red!—he wasn't prone to self-delusion. Andrea had known where he was in Sorrento for the past four days. The only variable still in play here was Seb's bullheadedness.

He'd bet on red and lost. Time to cash in his chips.

Chapter Fourteen

Toes dipping into
Tranquil waters like the tip
Of a lazy branch
-#118, *In Blue Solitudes*, S. Wilson-Osaki

One look at the sterile sheets of the small twin bed in his hotel room, and Seb bolted for the door. Halfway to the lobby, he thought twice about his attire, racing back to exchange his summer suit for a T-shirt and shorts, his dress sneaks for hiking runners, and his satchel for his backpack. Armed with a to-go cup of jet fuel—a triple espresso—and a restlessness he couldn't contain, Seb broke out into the starry Sorrento night.

He wandered for a while until he found himself on an old Roman road. Walled gardens on both sides kept the path narrow but direct. With only the moonlight as guide and companion, Seb dragged his fingers along the coarse fieldstone walls. Every so often, a peak-a-boo gate gave him a glimpse of the lush, overgrown gardens behind, the scent of jasmine wafting through the iron bars. He let the rhythm of his steps and the blanketing night lull him away from his conscious mind. Seb imagined himself a pilgrim journeying to a sacred site, bearing a sacrifice for an ancient god. He loved this place; everywhere he looked conjured an image of the past, as if that idyllic world was just a heartbeat away.

A fork in the road betrayed no evidence as to which way led down the road less travelled. Seb spotted an arrow sign with the word *Bar* painted in crude red letters. Jackpot. A raised path paralleled the coastline, its black rails almost invisible in the darkness. With only the moon glow off the slats, he followed the gleaming brick road until he came to the ruins of an ancient Roman villa. Through the vaulting archways, a dance of light beckoned. After a few false starts, he felt more than walked his way down to a hidden lagoon.

A tiny shingle beach looked toward a keyhole opening in the rock on the other side. Beyond, an unreachable horizon. Seb stood on the farthest stone of the beach, his toes hovering over the tranquil water. Communed with this secret place, where the earth cradled the sea. Every so often a surge from outside would stir the waters of the lagoon, like a mother reprimanding a complacent child. But then the tide would drain out again, and the surface would still. It would take a stronger hand to change this one's nature.

The red bar sign blinked in the back of Seb's mind as if lit in neon. His espresso buzz had been replaced by an ache only the balm of alcohol could dull. Seb dipped a stick in the water, wrote a quick haiku on the stones. It evaporated by the time he climbed back to the ruins, the strains of an Italian love song luring him to the topside bar.

Little more than a portable shack surrounded by deck chairs and two-seat tables, Seb was relieved to find it open. For such a remote spot, a surprising amount of people lounged around the bar and on the staggered rock shelves that led to the sea. While local couples kept well above the water line, a group of hikers gathered in a campfire circle on a nearby patch of brush. The strains of their guitars competed with the jazzy soundtrack piped in through the shack's two antennae-like speakers.

After placing his order, Seb settled into one of the farthest deck chairs to wait out the dawn. The drink of choice, a sweet *caipirinha* that bore little relation to its tart Brazilian cousin, went down smooth. When Sinatra's "Come Back to Sorrento" came on, Seb raised a toast to this hidden gem of a place, to the gorgeous city itself, to Capri in the distance, and to his time in Amalfi. He whispered words of gratitude to Henry and Andrea before downing the rest of his glass.

Despite the tightness in his throat, he waved at the bartender for a second round. Though he had several hours before checking out of his hotel, Seb clung to every minute lest it speed past, wishing he could halt the traffic of even this quiet corner of the world. Just stand at this intersection of his life with arms stretched out and a whistle between his lips, waiting for a sense of direction, for the claxon of inspiration.

Where did he go from here? Back to a house whose cold rooms echoed with happy memories? Back to friendships that were pantomimes of former intimacy? Back to his empty bed, to watching the stain of Henry's blood in the left lane of the Chemin Black get iced over by another endless winter? As if Seb had never been to this sun-burnished place. As if he'd never stolen through the gardens of an Amalfi villa to steal a kiss from one of the city's favorite sons.

He dug into his backpack for Henry's notebook. Skipping to the second-to-last page, Seb slipped out the letter he had paper-clipped back there; the one the executor gave him at the reading of Henry's will, along with the notebook and a few other treasures.

My heart,

I hope you never read this. I hope I'll toss it on the fire with old arthritic hands while sipping my last glass of shiraz. Or, if you are reading it, a ninety-five-year-old you is sitting on the sunny porch of the Italian villa where we've lived through our retirement years, surrounded by kids and grandkids and all the important people. Like Steph, who is forcing me to write this, just in case. I hate it—hate everything about it, except that it's for you—but she's right.

I'm no poet. You know that. I have some words, but you always had the best ones. The most eloquent, the most eviscerating. You're spellbinding, Seb. I want to listen to you forever. I want to say something perfect, something unforgettable. But if you're reading this, what is there to say but "I'm sorry"? I know I promised I would always come back. I fought to keep that promise. Please know that. Please forgive me.

I love you. I love you. I love you. When I got off the plane from my first trip to Amalfi and found you waiting for me at the gate, I knew. These are the notes from that trip, the beginning of our life together. I hope you'll read them, when you can. I hope you'll go back there to find me. I'm waiting for you, my heart, on the steps of the Duomo. If you look into the crowd, you'll see me there.

Forever yours,
Henry

Seb carefully folded the note, slid it into his wallet. Settled in to read. From page one, line one, to the last doodle, he followed Henry's every scribble, draft, half-formed notion. Thought about his adventures with a swell of pride when he reached passages that had guided him. Seb had managed to hit more of the recommended sites than he'd missed. Better still, Amalfi had sunk into his bones. He loved it the way Henry had loved it, heartache and all.

When the first glimmers of sunlight pinked the horizon, Seb borrowed a knife from the bar. After slicing out the pages with personal significance and stashing them in his writing journal, Seb stared at the notebook awhile, longer at the view.

A soft peck to the cover; a murmured farewell. Leaving Henry's notebook on the slim table for the next traveler to find, Seb embarked on the long journey home.

An argument of operatic ferocity blasted Seb as he lugged his suitcase down the main staircase of the Villa dei D'Armiento, an eighteenth-century hotel modernized by an adorable family into a camera-ready Hollywood dream of a place. The personal touch the website promised meant they were occasionally short on staff. The two lovely ladies at the front desk, Maria and Nina, were so demure and accommodating that the fact that they held their own against whatever belligerent fat cat currently attempted to throw his weight around shocked Seb. Until he turned the corner into the lobby and discovered the not-so-fat cat in question was Andrea.

"What's going on here?" Seb demanded, abandoning his bag.

"*O Santo Dio!*" Andrea kissed his fingertips, raised them to the sky. "Sebastiano…" Andrea reached out in his direction, but some internal hesitation kept him from taking a step.

Possibly the look on Seb's face, which he'd set to "murder with your eyes."

"*Signor* Osaki, this gentleman"—Nina—or Maria?—seemed to doubt her own appraisal—"insists to speak with you. He doesn't have a room number, and you left no instructions…"

"You did the right thing," Seb reassured them. "Will you watch my bag? I'll be back in a minute." Halfway to the back exit, he realized Andrea hadn't followed him. "Come on."

Seb tried not to let the look of relief that washed over Andrea's face get to him. Andrea sped after him like a scolded puppy but gave him space once outside. Mermaid's tail-patterned tiles scaled out to a palm grove. Seb led them down the path toward the pool, out of earshot of any early morning risers.

When he glanced back at Andrea, Seb found him leaning on the whitewashed Victorian lamppost as if he needed to catch his breath. Bruise eyed and clumsily shaven, Seb recognized the hunted cast to his visage all too well. The glossy waves of his hair were slicked back in a pompadour

Seb hadn't glimpsed since the day he landed. His vet's uniform, a crisp white dress shirt and ass-hugging jeans, replaced the team colors Andrea usually wore. He looked officious, choirboy penitent, and like he hadn't slept in a week.

Seb resisted the urge to smother him with affection. Or strangle him where he stood. To release all expectations and just listen. Trouble was Seb didn't know what he wanted to hear.

And Andrea, for all the ruckus he'd caused, didn't know what to say. Twice he raised his hands, opened his mouth, only to fold back in on himself—a conductor who'd lost his tempo. The nervous stutter of his foot tapping the tiles made Seb take some pity on him.

"You left me."

Wounded eyes found his, locked in. "You looked so perfect, bundled in the covers. In my arms. My sleeping beauty. And I knew that everything that was to come over the next few days, it would never be as perfect. When you were in Amalfi, I could push away the thought that you would leave soon… but here, in Sorrento, I would know. Every minute I would know. And I didn't trust myself not to…"

"Not to…?"

"Be selfish."

"You think leaving without saying goodbye wasn't selfish?"

Andrea let out a blustery sigh. "I know. I dropped off my last client that day, and I was sick in the street. All I could think of was you, but I wasn't *thinking* of you. Does that make sense?"

"No."

"Then I remembered about Henry and..." Seb struggled to be unmoved by the telltale glisten in Andrea's eyes. "I am so, so sorry. I am a worm. I am a *scarafaggio*, one of those little—"

"Ostriches." All the more endearing with crow's feet and crinkled brow, apparently.

"Is that an insect?"

"Bird. Gigantic thing. Likes to stick its head in the sand to hide from predators."

"Ah. Then yes, I am an ostrich. A very apologetic ostrich."

"I can see that." Seb padded over to him, caught one of his hands. "Fortunately this kitsune is rather partial to big, floppy, skittish birds."

"Kit... what?"

"Shapeshifting fox from Japanese mythology."

Andrea managed a hard-earned smirk. "I would have thought an Arctic fox since—"

"Don't say it. We do have four seasons in Canada, you know."

"Then I'll have to make sure I visit in summer." Andrea squeezed his hand so hard Seb thought he'd heard a crack. "If I'm still invited?"

He pretended to think it over for so long Andrea kicked his foot.

"Ow! Hey! Do you always abuse people you're begging forgiveness from?"

"I don't know about begging..." The melancholy tinge

to Andrea's expression wasn't very playful or convincing.

"We'll save that for next time." Even Seb couldn't summon up a convincingly seductive tone. "Come here." He pulled Andrea into a straightjacket hug, nesting his cheek in that stiff, citrus-scented pompadour until he felt him begin to shudder. Then he held him even tighter. "I missed you, you *stronzo*."

A muffled laugh tickled his collarbone. Andrea cleared his throat several times before raising his head but made no move to break their embrace.

"Let me drive you to the airport. All the way to Rome, if you want."

"How do you know I'm going to Rome?"

"I checked the flights to Montreal."

Seb gazed deep into sincere, aching eyes and decided to indulge his inner kitsune.

"Okay. But there better be a *granita al limone* in my future."

"Only the best when you ride with me."

Fifteen minutes later, armed with a *granita* and a homemade *sfogliatella* courtesy of a care package from Vina, Seb sunk into the swank leather of the SUV's passenger seat for what he hoped was not the last time. Andrea revved the car to life but paused before shifting her into gear.

"Airport or Rome?"

"Just head for the highway."

Seb could tell he wanted to object, but his kind, considerate, quick-tempered, skittish, giving sweep of a man couldn't bring himself to say a word against someone he had so recently wronged. Yet another thing Seb admired about him. As they navigated the tight streets and those stomach-sinking corners, Seb waited for Andrea to say something, make some kind of move. To fight for what Seb knew he wanted. Andrea's head may have no longer been in the sand, but that didn't make him a bird of prey.

"So... you went to Fabiana's."

"I did." Surprised by the change of subject, Seb shifted so he could look at him. "I wanted to spend my last night in Italy in the place that had brought me the most joy."

He didn't think he imagined Andrea tightening his grip on the steering wheel.

"She said that you had a talk with Bruno."

Seb scoffed. "More like Bruno talked *at* me. That guy does not understand the meaning of personal space."

"Did he hurt you?"

"No, no. Just..." Seb took a long slurp of his drink as he gathered his thoughts. "I wish him well, so long as he stays away from me."

Andrea snorted. "He has that effect on people." A nervous twitch fluttered the edge of Andrea's eyelid. Seb sensed he fought to keep his focus on the road. "I was with Federica when *Zia* Fabi called. Otherwise—"

"It's all right."

He slammed his palm into the steering wheel. "No, it's not!"

"You apologized. I accepted. You brought pastries. There's nothing left to say."

The SUV swerved into an alleyway, screeched to a halt at the end of a cul de sac five paces from a dead-drop cliff. Andrea punched the gear into park, whipped off his seat belt. He crawled so far over the seat divider that he was practically in Seb's lap. After clicking open the passenger door, he gave it a hard shove.

"Out!"

Seb barely had time to stow the last few bites of his *sfogliatella* before Andrea bulldozed him into the road. Abandoning the SUV with the keys still in the ignition, Andrea grabbed Seb by the arm, tugging him over to a tight square of space between the back of an apartment building and the cliffside rail.

"Where are we going?"

"I don't want to do this in that fucking car."

Andrea eased Seb back against the coarse stucco wall. A lightning strike of gray-and-green flashes fired in his eyes. He closed in on Seb, sparking the air between them. Cupping his face, Andrea kissed him deeply, desperately, as if only a breath away from unleashing a hurricane of emotion. Seb surrendered to the storm.

"I can't lose you." Andrea's frantic breaths gusted down the slope of Seb's neck, tingling with promise.

"You won't."

"You say that now, but I've seen it so many times. People make promises when they're in the thick of it, but once they're home…" Another seismic kiss. "I know you're still figuring out how to… to exist without your husband, but… Ah, Sebastiano. I'm falling in love with you."

Seb beamed at him, wanting—absurdly—to cheer. To shout. To fly the team colors with pride. His sweep, from way behind the half line, had finally scored.

Instead Seb took his mouth, pouring all his jumbled but

ardent emotions into their embrace. When they finally came up for air, he whispered, "I think it's time you took me home."

Andrea recoiled as if he'd been shot. He wrenched out of Seb's arms, bolted back to the SUV. Seb chased after him, cursing his choice of words.

"Wait. Dre—" Seb grabbed for him, but he leapt through the passenger door and across the divider.

"Get in." The roar of the engine drowned out Seb's second plea. "You'll miss your flight."

"I'm not—"

"Airport," Andrea choked out, "or Rome?"

Seb leaned in through the passenger seat, his feet planted on the ground so Andrea couldn't speed away. He'd almost lost him once. Never again.

"Amalfi." He covered Andrea's hand with his own. "Take me home to Amalfi, Dre."

Andrea fell back into his seat with a dull thud. He gaped at Seb, who peeled his fingers off the clutch, twined them with his own. Seb reached over, Andrea's eyes following him as he clicked the SUV back into park and killed the ignition.

"Come on. Out again."

Seb ran over to the driver's side in time to catch Andrea when he staggered out. He gathered him in a loose hug so that they could look out to the sea. A view so epic and indelible Seb knew he would never tire of it. Much like the man in his arms.

Who'd finally recovered enough from his shock to formulate a question.

"What do you mean, 'home'? What have you done?"

"Called Vincenzo this morning. Lucky for me, he had a cancellation. I've got a spot at the Villa Napolitana for the next two weeks, which will give us enough time to find me an apartment. I will have to go back to Montreal at some point to pick up Nagiko and whatever I'll need. But I can stay for at least six months. By then I figure we'll know if I need to look into something more… permanent." Seb gazed hopefully into his stoic Roman face. "That is, if all that's okay with you?"

"You, Amalfi, our home?" Andrea broke out his luminous smile. "Everything about that, about you, is okay with me, Sebastiano."

He melted into Andrea's embrace, his whole body lit by the fire of his kiss, by the gentleness of his spirit, by the promise of a boundless future.

Acknowledgements

In 2015, for one of those big "0" birthdays, I gifted myself a trip to the Amalfi Coast, a place so beautiful and so romantic it almost defies description. Being a writer, I had to at least try to put my experience into words. Seb's story came to me on one of my many ferry rides between towns. Travelling by water requires its own kind of Zen, but I came to love it, along with, as you might have noticed, everything else about the place. If you have a chance to go there, do. It's one of the jewels of the world.

This book would not have been possible without the encouragement and infinite patience of my editor, Nancy-Anne Davies, who deserves an extra thank-you for taking the reins on the foaling scene. I adore my betas, Karen Wellsbury, Liv Rancourt, Day's Lee, and Judie Troyansky, whose early support of the book helped me see that I could indeed write contemporary. G&Ts for everyone! My cover artist, the Lady Tiferet, is both cheerleader and security blanket. Knowing she's going to bibbidy-bobbidy-boo the book into something gorgeous and marketable gives me no end of confidence.

A massive thank-you to my sensitivity readers Francesca Borzi, Melanie Ting, and Koji Takahashi for their insights and corrections. It means the world to me that they were willing to share their life experiences/culture with me. Any mistakes that might have crept in there are my fault alone.

Share Your Experience

If you enjoyed this book, please consider leaving a review on the site where you purchased it, or on GoodReads.

Thank you for your support of independent authors!

Books by Selina Kray

Like Stars

Stoker & Bash: The Fangs of Scavo

Stoker & Bash: The Fruit of the Poisonous Tree (coming 2018)

About the Author

Selina Kray is the nom de plume of an author and English editor. Professionally she has covered all the artsy-fartsy bases, having worked in a bookstore, at a cinema, in children's television, and in television distribution, up to her latest incarnation as a subtitle editor and grammar nerd (though she may have always been a grammar nerd). A self-proclaimed geek and pop culture junkie who sometimes manages to pry herself away from the review sites and gossip blogs to write fiction of her own, she is a voracious consumer of art with both a capital and lowercase A.

Selina's aim is to write genre-spanning romances with intricate plots, complex characters, and lots of heart. Whether she has achieved this goal is for you, gentle readers, to decide. At present she is hard at work on future novels at home in Montreal, Quebec, with her wee corgi serving as both foot warmer and in-house critic.

If you're interested in receiving Selina's newsletter and being the first to know when new books are released, plus getting sneak peeks at upcoming novels, please sign up at her website: www.selinakray.net

Find Selina online:
Twitter: @selinakray
Facebook: facebook.com/people/Selina-Kray/100009929464776
Google+: plus.google.com/104484914913249635905
GoodReads: goodreads.com/author/show/9853715.Selina_Kray
Email: selinakray@hotmail.ca
Website: www.selinakray.net

faeces 4, 5
fart 10
fasting 6, 62
fat 3, 14, 71
fatty acids 8, 12
  short chain 27, 39
fatty foods 59
fennel 63
fermentation 4, 8, 14, 27, 42, 52, 68
fizzy drinks 72
flatulence 59
flatus 8, 10, 15, 27, 68
food combining 25, 60
fried foods 59
fructans 15
fructose 15, 48, 49, 52, 69
fruits 52, 53, 71
fullness 3

galactopinitol 40
gall bladder 3
gall stones 34
garlic 24, 38, 63, 64, 65, 73
gas 6, 7, 11
gas, measurement of 68
gas, production of 10, 13
gas, volume of 4, 10, 11, 16, 22, 35
  in men 16, 23
  in women 16, 23
gases, smelly 14, 23, 57, 58, 63, 64
gastroenteritis 46
glucose 48, 49
grape juice 49
greenhouse gases 18
gurgles 70

haemorrhoids 19
Hay Diet 60
heartburn 36, 74
herbs 63, 64
hiatus hernia 36, 75
hiccups 79
honey 50
hormone replacement therapy 17
hormones 16
hunger 3
hydrogen 7, 13, 16, 23, 24, 27, 32, 33, 54, 61, 63, 68
  breath tests for 68
hydrogen sulphide 23, 27, 43, 58, 63

ice cream 28, 45
idli 42
indole 57, 63
infants 46, 76
inulin 29
irritable bowel syndrome 11, 35, 66

jams 50
juices 24, 50
  fruit 49

lactase 45
lactose 38, 45, 48, 68
lactose intolerance 28, 29, 45, 68
large intestine 4
leeks 38
legumes 41
lignin 4

maltose 48
manganese 41
manninotriose 40
mannitol 51
meat 14, 57
men 16, 23
mercaptans 43, 63
methane 7, 16, 18, 23, 26, 27, 32, 33, 47, 61, 63
methyl sulphides 43, 63
milk 28, 38, 45, 69
mood 33
mountaineers 30
mucins 61, 62
mushrooms 64
mustard seeds 40, 41

nitrogen 7, 13, 24, 61, 73
noise 19

odour 7, 16, 43
oesophagus 1, 36, 74
oligosaccharides 27, 40, 41, 42, 60, 61
onions 15, 24, 38, 63, 64, 73
orange juice 49
orange peel 56
oxygen 7, 73

pain 20, 31, 35, 37, 45, 76
pancreas 3, 64

pancreatic juice 3
pear juice 49
pectin 52, 53, 56
peptic ulcer 64
pineapple juice 49
pinitol 40
polyp 64
possetting 76
potato crisps 24
potatoes 12
preservatives 24
progestogen 17
protein 1, 3, 14, 24, 25, 60, 63, 64, 71
prune juice 49
Pujol, Joseph 25

raffinose 27, 40, 41, 42
rectum 4, 10, 22
reflux 1, 75
regurgitation 76
resistant starch 54, 62
rice 71
rotten egg gas 63
rumblings 70, 71, 72

saliva 1
scuba divers 31
seeds 38
   mustard 40, 41
   sprouting 61
short chain fatty acids 27, 39
shrimp 63
skatole 57, 63
small intestine 3, 4, 7
smelly gases 14, 23, 57, 58, 63, 64
sodium metabisulphite 24
sorbitol 49, 50, 69
soya beans 40, 41
soya milk 28
spices 14, 29, 63, 64
sprouting 41, 61

stachyose 27, 40, 42
starch 1, 4, 8, 23, 27, 54
   resistant 54, 62
stomach 1, 2, 3, 7
stomach acid 1, 36
stools 39
   floating 47
stress 74
sucrose 48, 69
sugars 3, 8, 23, 27, 48
sulphides 23
sulphur 58, 64
sulphur compounds 15, 23, 43, 65, 73
sulphur-containing foods 24
sulphur dioxide 7
swallowed air 1, 7, 9, 24, 38, 62, 75, 76, 77, 78

tempeh 41–2
tension 13, 33, 72
therapies 28
tofu 42
transit time 4, 16, 26
   in men 4, 5
   in women 4, 5
trisulphides 43
turbulence 70
turnips 38, 43

vegetables 29, 71
verbascose 27, 40, 42
vomiting 75

wine 24
women 16, 23

X-ray 68

yeast 44
yoghurt 45, 47